When Becomes Night

Ghost Stories

By

Graeme Milne

Published by Landon Press

First Edition

Cover Design: Cruzzcreation

Cover Photograph: The author

ISBN 978-1-915787-93-4

Dedication

To my dear friend Steve Morrison, sadly no longer with us. An aficionado of ghost stories and all things esoteric. I hope you would approve.

Table of Contents

Bad Energy

'Well Steven, this is Alex McIntyre,' said the doctor indicating with his hand the pale figure who sat opposite him. Steven, the younger doctor of the two stepped forward and proffered a hand but the figure sitting cross legged upon the bed did not reciprocate. Doctor Bromley appeared unconcerned and continued his introduction. 'Mr. McIntyre, has been with us just over a year and has made great in-roads since his arrival. I'm sure Mr McIntyre won't mind me saying, that it took some months for him to settle, but I do believe we have now turned a corner.' He glanced towards his patient for approval, but the mans, sullen expression gave nothing away. Bromley looked a little downhearted, before asking his patient if he had slept well. The man however remained silent, the dark circles under his eyes suggesting otherwise. Steven who had literally just arrived and was currently being given the grand tour of his new workplace scrutinised the patient intently. He assumed Alex to be in his mid-thirties though the light smattering of hair valiantly attempting to cover his dome made him look

1

older as did the equally sparse growth lurking upon his chin. He was a poorly looking specimen his frailty enhanced by a dressing gown which was at least two sizes too large for him. Hanging in folds his stick like arms, hairless and pale poked from its voluminous sleeves and at the end of those arms a pair of milk white hands fidgeted. They were, Steven surmised, the only part of his anatomy in which life's essence appeared to flow, so it came as a surprise when moments later he broke his silence.

'I am not sleeping particularly well, to be honest,' he stated flatly while continuing to stare at the corner of the room. After a short silence, he continued. 'I did as you suggested and turned the radio off before bed.'

Bromley nodded slowly, 'and how long has it been since the last incident?' The question hung in the air like smoke but received no answer. Bromley turned to his companion. 'I should point out that Mr McIntyre likes to listen to the radio at night, he finds it calming.' The patient nodded imperceptibly while continuing to gaze into the far corner of the room. Upon listening a faint sound could be heard coming from the direction of his gaze. Bromley frowned and stepping forward opened the drawer of a nearby cabinet discovering the source of his fixation. It was a radio, and the room instantly filled with the inane babble of an over excited pundit. The elder of the two wrinkled his nose in disgust and after turning the dial closed the drawer with a sigh.

'I see you are listening to the football, Alex. I didn't know you were a fan, what team do you follow?'

'None' came the tart reply, 'the only thing that concerns me is the volume, what's playing is irrelevant to me.' Steven glanced towards his superior who if offended did not show it.

'Well, Alex, we must be heading off,' said Bromley after a brief pause. 'People to visit, places to see, I'm sure you and Steven will get to know each other soon enough.' Whether a response was expected remained a moot point as Alex continued to stare towards the corner of the room his head tilted slightly as if listening for something. Outside Bromley confided in him. 'McIntyre is an obsessive insisting on always having background noise around him. Come this way, I would like to share his story with you. It is an interesting case. In the time he has been here he has made some progress, but...,' his voice trailed off as he took a sharp right.

On catching him up, the doctor continued. 'He believes that he can communicate with ghosts or at least they communicate with him. The background noise from the radio for example allows him to function without hearing their presence, or so he believes. It's a fascinating story which I am certain will intrigue you, but lets' wait till we get to the office.' Continuing their way, the loud clip of their heels now echoed in the confines of the corridor. Steven struggling to keep up felt a twinge of annoyance at their frenetic pace, barely having time to take in his surroundings though what he saw was as expected. It was a Victorian institution, an asylum back in the day and no amount of art could disguise the fact, to call it austere would have been an understatement. Still despite his misgivings, as a newly qualified doctor with little experience, he considered himself lucky to have been offered the position in the first place.

Without warning Bromley halted and in doing so produced an impressive set of keys with which he opened his office door. Inside Steven was met by the sight of a meticulously arranged room. On the left two comfortable chairs sat facing each other separated by a large green leather-topped desk, while on the right a battered leather sofa lay directly in front of the door. Upon it sat a large bundle of blankets, draped across its headrest. 'Sleepover night for me I'm afraid, thus the blankets,' smiled Bromley on noticing Steven's inquisitive look. 'How often do you have to stay over?' enquired Steven in response. 'Not too often, thankfully,' replied the other, 'I can never quite settle unless I'm in my own bed and can't function without a proper sleep. There's nothing like your own bed, don't you agree? Steven nodded; however, his attention was drawn to the large cast iron fireplace at the far end of the room. It was beautifully moulded but seemed a little uninviting its cavernous mouth crying out for flame. In front of it sat a reading chair and within grabbing distance a large oak bookcase wherein sat impressive row of books. Steven approached with reverence and murmured his appreciation.

His reverie was interrupted at the sound of Bromley's voice. 'I see you are looking at my collection,' and without waiting for a reply, continued. 'I do love books, in fact that is one thing we have in common, that is myself and Alex I mean.' He continued. 'Our mutual interest has proven a great distraction on several occasions, especially when our conversations have begun to chase their tails.' Steven murmured though his eyes continued to drink in the titles. It was an interesting collection ranging from the obligatory classic textbooks to volumes on the great artists. There were also as numerous titles on more esoteric subjects which caused Steven to momentarily raise his brows. As if reading his mind Bromley continued, 'I have found it useful to arm myself with as much knowledge as possible. 'World mysteries, religions, the whole concept of belief holds a certain fascination for me, but as a doctor and a pragmatist I can't say I subscribe to many of the ideas within. Nevertheless, it has helped me in the treatment of some of my patients over the years. Would you like coffee?'

'Yes, that would be great,' replied Steven.

'And how have you found your first morning? Bromley enquired, as he busied himself pouring the drinks.

'I must admit, I have found it a little overwhelming,' said Steven.

Bromley let out a deep sigh before answering. 'It can be, it can be, but rest assured you will only be given a small number of patients to keywork at first.' Gesturing for Steven to take a seat he continued. 'Anyway, as you have no doubt gathered, Alex's case is a fascinating one and deserves further explanation. I have worked with him for over a year now and would like to think that in that time I have got to know him reasonably well. I see him every day as a matter of course. When he first arrived things were different, and it took him around a month to talk coherently about the events which led to his eventual hospitalisation. Since his arrival I have kept his case notes up to date and it is those I wish to share now.' After briefly sipping his coffee, Bromley began.

'The facts pertaining to the breakdown of Alex McIntyre were undoubtedly due to a combination of factors and in many ways his own beliefs. A complex man he is inquisitive, sensitive and by his own admission has an obsessive streak. Before his illness he enjoyed a wide range of interests, though tended to be solitary in his pursuits. When he came to us last

May he was in a frantic state. It took weeks of rest and medication before he was able to give a coherent semblance of the facts leading up to his breakdown. He readily admitted in our ensuing meetings that his 'obsessions' as he called them were the cause of his present condition. These included researching historic crimes, particularly one infamous murder case of which you are no doubt familiar. The case known throughout the world, due in no small part to the name of its main protagonist literally haunted him. Perhaps it was the horrific nature of the crimes or the fact he was never caught but either way it obsessed him. Strangely, when pressed on the subject he still never refers to the killer by name, preferring to discuss the murders in more oblique terms, calling them 'incidents,' or the perpetrator as 'the man in red'. After hearing the facts, you might understand why he does this.'

The young Doctor flashed a quizzical look, to which his mentor responded. 'In a nutshell, he believes that the mere mention of the perpetrators name can attract him.

'In what way?' replied Steven somewhat confused.

Bromley, placing his fingers upon his chin thought for a moment before continuing. 'To be blunt, he believes the killers name, whose *nom de plume* was conjured up by the fevered mind of a salacious hack should never be mentioned at all costs.'

Stevens look of bemusement prompted Bromley to continue. 'He is, by his own admission, superstitious, overly sensitive, and prone to dwelling on morbid subjects. He came to believe, through a deep-seated interest in spiritualism, that the power of his mind could attract and repel tangible manifestations according to his thoughts. I know you might find this whole subject to be bordering on nonsensical, but I can assure you he fervently believes that this is the case. I of course, believe in what I can see, and touch though I have over the course of the last year made a concerted effort to study as much as I can on the subject. Suffice to say that my own once unshakeable beliefs have at the very least trembled on occasion though I am slightly embarrassed to admit this. Despite Stevens incredulous look he continued, 'I have on more than one occasion while in the presence of McIntyre witnessed things that have, shall we say, opened my mind.'

The younger man interrupted, 'What do you mean? He created something physical out of thin air by using the power of his mind.

A slight sheen of perspiration now peppered Bromley's forehead and after wiping it with a nearby tissue he continued. 'There is a belief in certain religions, particularly spiritualism, that sensitive people can draw energy from places where they should best remain. They claim to be able to connect with the afterlife and that through meditation and adherence to a few simple rules one can journey to other realms and connect with those who have died. I am, as you are, a man whose understanding of the world is based upon provable facts so to me these theories were nothing more than fantasy. In our sessions he often argued that energy never dies but lives on. We often discussed this subject and if it were not accorded enough gravitas, he would become vociferous and angry, I suppose through frustration at his own unfortunate predicament. He ranted that the general masses were mere savages, never happier than when devouring pie and mash in front of the TV or sinking pints before the match. He went on to suggest that man could never evolve and reach his true potential unless willing to accept the concept of spiritual development. On questioning he would often end up sulking and many of our sessions would end with him refusing to speak further.'

'Was he always this way?' asked Steven after a short interval.

'Apparently so, even as a child or whether collecting comics in his youth the same pattern always emerged. He would commit wholly to his pursuits until the phase had run its course or he became bored. For example, as an adult he took an interest in spiritualism which slowly developed from reading on the subject. This graduated to weekly meetings at the local church where, with a small select band of like-minded souls he would sit and listen to lectures on spiritualist history and spirit photography.' Bromley stopped for a moment, his lips puckering at the rim of his cup, but having second thoughts he continued.

'Over time he became convinced of the existence of another dimension which could neither be seen nor heard until under the right conditions, and that he could communicate with this hidden world. He believed he was able to take these small spiritual journeys at the drop of a hat, if the fancy took him. He also believed that these journeys came with a price and that when he returned to the now, he was not entirely alone. He began to feel afraid, and his sleep was disrupted by vivid dreams. On more than one occasion he slept with the light on, convinced that someone else was with him.'

Steven shifted in his seat. 'May, I top up?' He enquired, indicating the cafetiere.

'Why of course, here let me.' The Doctor lent forward and replenished their cups before sitting back heavily. Steven noticed disappointingly, that in the interim the liquid had cooled somewhat, but keen to hear more asked him to continue.

'According to what I was told, things took a more sinister turn soon after when fate led him to a local bookshop. Scanning the shelves his eyes alighted on a newly published tome about a series of gruesome murders which took place some hundred years ago. It had been solved or so the author proclaimed and being on a subject which interested him he began to flick through the pages. In the middle a series of shocking images jolted his brain, images he remembered as a child on chancing upon a similar book.' Bromley shifted in his seat before continuing.

'Despite his repulsion he ended up buying the book and once home devoured the contents and so a pattern then emerged. Further visits to the bookshop secured fresh reading material and soon a small library on the subject formed. Who was the killer? Why had he never been caught? Numerous theories had been put forward and Alex apparently read every one to get to the truth. His sleep patterns then became disrupted. Soon after he described to me how he began to feel he was not alone though at first, he shrugged it off as his overactive imagination. This changed one evening when he fell asleep on the sofa waking soon after at the sound of material swishing near his face. He awoke with a start, the image of voluminous skirts trailing across cobbles imprinted on his mind. From that day onward he did not sleep well and at night would habitually lie in bed staring into the darkness, listening. He could not say what he was listening out for, but he felt sure he was not alone. Sometimes he could hear faint voices, on other occasions he sensed subtle movements in the furthest corners of his room. These odd occurrences, imperceptible yet always there only added to his dread. He began forming a protective circle of light in his mind to keep at bay what he claimed now circled him in the dark. Eventually the soft whisperings and rustlings became too much and so he began to play the radio in order to drown out their sounds, which as you have seen, he continues to do.'

'Did he find that it helped in any way?' asked Steven.

'To a point,' replied Bromley, 'but after a while he became paranoid about what he was now unable to hear. He became obsessed with the idea that he had somehow opened a metaphoric door and the constant strain resulted in his mental collapse.

'Dr Bromley, you mentioned earlier that you had started to believe in some elements of his story, is this true?'

Bromley's brow furrowed and looking momentarily embarrassed replied. 'I wouldn't quite say that. What I implied, was that I adopted a more open-minded approach to his story.'

'Why?' pressed Steven.

The doctor looked a little flustered and for the first time his voice lost a little of its authority. 'Well, I suppose having heard his story so often I felt it had affected me in some way. It was because of something he said….' His voice trailed off, but Steven continued to press.

'Such as?' enquired his companion.

'I don't mind telling you, in fact I will be glad to, but first let me finish telling you about McIntyre.' Steven nodded and bade his time.

'As I mentioned earlier it took some time before he felt well enough to divulge the circumstances leading to his breakdown and I think it's better you hear them in his own words.' With that he rose and taking a tape recorder from a nearby drawer, placed it in front of Steven. He then opened the bottom drawer of his desk before holding a cassette up to the light. As if determining the quality of a rare gem he held it aloft for some seconds before placing it into the player. He smiled benignly as the tape then hissed into life. It was Bromley's voice who introduced the session and a few moments later a flat voice began to speak. It was Alex, his monotone delivery instantly recognisable.

'I remember I had turned the radio off and was lying in the silence, my body floating in space. I had to try and sleep, but the darkness felt solid and was alive with white noise. The more I tried to ignore it, the more intrusive it became and although I must have dozed off at some point, I was soon being drawn back to full wakefulness. It was now silent. I glanced to my left and noticed on the clock it had just gone one. I kept staring upwards and the ceiling slowly formed as my eyes grew accustomed to the dark. I felt a sense of apprehension and found myself scrutinizing the room. I didn't want to look, but I couldn't stop myself. In the corner, where the bookcase stood, I thought I saw a long shape standing next to it. I remember rubbing my eyes, but the shape remained. It was dark and I couldn't quite make it out, but it looked out of place. I screwed up my eyes, then realising my feet were poking out of the covers I drew them in slowly.

I felt like I did as a kid, always worried something would grab at my feet should they stray too far from the quilt. I suppose most kids are like that. It was then I thought I heard a noise but when I listened it stopped. Soon after it started again, it wasn't that loud, but it was there, a sort of rustling sound like dry leaves. There was now an unpleasant tingling sensation running across my skin and as I glanced around the room, I saw the bookcase again but now there was no shape next to it. That's when I got scared and I remember looking to my right and God help me, saw the shape standing at the foot of my bed. There was a faint clucking noise coming from its direction. Soon the strange glottal sound had increased in volume, and I could hear in my head an insidious soft voice crooning some old-time nonsense. It was as if I were being held in a trance and I could only blink, my body unable to move. The figure then began to climb onto my bed, and I shrank from it, burrowing back into the mattress. I could feel my organs crashing internally like a deranged orchestra. It was without doubt a female presence and she now lay or floated above me; I couldn't tell which. Her face still hidden by the dark now hovered mere inches above me and I prayed that it remained hidden knowing what she would look like. I can still remember the rasping sound of her breathing which slowly degenerated to that of air escaping bellows. It was then something wet and sticky dropped onto my cheek and as it tickled towards my chin, I launched myself upwards convinced I would concuss myself against whatever it was, but I encountered only air. I then clicked the light on but found nothing, nothing but the familiar. I kept the light on for the remainder of the night. I didn't ask for this, I couldn't stop myself from thinking.' At that moment Bromley lent forward and switching the recording faced his companion.

'Of course, one could easily put this down to a bad dream or sleep paralysis. We all have nightmares from time to time and certainly dwelling on things is not good for one's well-being, as you well know. Anyhow there is one more recording I would like you to hear,' and with that he retrieved another tape. Seconds later the same tired voice filled the room.

'After three nights without sleep I destroyed all my books connected to the case. It must have been the beginning of July, but I can't remember the exact date. Things are a little vague, but I must have felt anxious and decided to go outside for some air. It would have been about ten or eleven in the evening or thereabouts. It was just beginning to get dark so it must have been around that time. I was standing in the back lane and lit a cigarette. The air was warm, and I distinctly remember seeing a small bat fly up and down the lane. Yes, I remember the bat. They always came out in late summer. On seeing it my mind eased momentarily and I cannot describe how good it felt. It was then I became aware of a soft crunching coming from further down the lane. I thought at first it was one of the neighbours taking their dog for a last-minute walk. I glanced down the lane but could barely make out who it was, the area being lost in shadow. A moment later I noticed that the figure was heading towards me and as it got closer, I could tell it was a woman. It was then I realised that parts of her were missing. I began to fumble with the gate but before I could open it, she was standing next to me. I think, she smiled and then touched me...' The tape then clicked off without warning.

'And that is where it ends.' Remarked Bromley. 'He has no recollection from then on in. We know from the police report that his terrified screams brought a few brave souls running and on finding him, there was no option but to contact the hospital. He was under sedation for weeks and any attempt to find out what happened was met with hysteria. Of course, thankfully he is now able to communicate.

Steven rubbed his jaw. 'Is he likely to get over this?'

'Possibly, but it will take time' sighed the older man. 'Which brings me to my point. I was hoping that a fresh pair of ears might help and so, forgive me for the cloak and dagger approach, but I am gifting you Mr McIntyre.' Steven's eyebrows raised.

'Don't be alarmed', said Bromley, acknowledging the others concern, 'I can assure you there is nothing sinister at play. I have worked with him for some considerable time and frankly he is most likely fed up with me. Perhaps it may be conducive that you step in for the moment.'

Steven sipped at his coffee which had gone disappointingly cold, before replying. 'I am more than happy to work with him but there is one thing I must ask. You mentioned a certain incident some time ago which involved you both. Would you mind telling me what happened.'

'Why of course, I have no issue with that at all,' replied Bromley, 'but you must promise that it goes no further than these four walls. Some of my colleagues who are not *au fait* with the case might well find room for mockery. I am quite proud of my reputation and would prefer it remained untarnished. It would be a professional courtesy.'

'Why of course, I wouldn't dream of….' But the doctor had already started.

'Around seven months ago I was on one of my bi-weekly visits and during our session I made an off-the-cuff remark regarding his morbid interests. It was nothing that anyone in the full grip of their faculties would take umbrage over, however Alex flew into a terrible sulk. He refused to accept my apology and instead said, that if I was so damn sure of myself, and disbelieved everything he had told me, then he would prove it by asking someone to pay me a visit. The idea was preposterous, but he said it with such conviction that I felt the skin on my neck goose instantly. I am ashamed to say I ordered a little extra medication for our friend that evening. I know it was spiteful, but I was angry, and a horribly depressive mood hung around me all day. As duty doctor, I then had to settle in for the night, a pleasure you will no doubt have to participate in soon.' Steven smiled.

'It was around a week before Christmas, and I remember it quite clearly as I had a coal fire on and soon drifted off to sleep on the sofa you see behind you. I must have slept for some time as the grate was near black apart from a faint glow when I wakened. My attention was drawn to the bookcase and as my eyes grew accustomed to the dark, I became convinced that there was someone else in the room. Whoever it was stood in the recess right next to the bookcase. It was a strange, lumped shape and though I stared at it for what seemed minutes, I can still not describe it adequately. It was then that it moved and with that I heard a rush of skirts. I then lunged for the light and afterwards drank coffee like it was going out of fashion. It goes without saying I did not sleep a wink for the rest of the night. Obviously, it had been a nightmare.' Bromley's then trailed off sounding unconvinced at his own diagnosis.

15

'Has it happened again?' enquired Steven after a discreet amount of time.

'Well, only now and then, but it's merely a bad dream and in our line of work I'm surprised we don't have more. One can be a sponge for some of the horror stories we hear, I imagine. Anyhow when morning came, I met with the doctor on morning duty and did a final check before handing over. It was then that McIntyre asked if I "had enjoyed the visit." I knew he was playing mind games with me and so I chose to ignore it. A week later he apologised for his actions and swore he would never do the same again and since then has been a model patient. I must admit though the incident did rattle me a little. Of course, it was my imagination, after all we work long hours.' Bromley lifted the cafetière towards Steven. 'More coffee?'

'No, thank you. I think I would like to read over his files though, if that all right. I'm quite keen to find out more.'

'Of course, of course,' said Bromley, clapping his hands together. 'I can get you them presently,' and with that the doctor rose from his chair and busied himself at the filing cabinet. Steven stretched, it had been a long day and stifling a yawn he too rose. It was then he became aware of the sudden noise that filled the room. It was a radio, and the sound of inane chatter now assailed his ears. Bromley quickly fiddled with the dial and several seconds later the sound of classical music took over. 'Ah! that's better,' he sighed. He turned towards Steven and on noticing his puzzlement added, 'I must admit, I do enjoy listening to the radio, especially at night', and with that he continued to search for the file.

Debris

Taking a deep breath, Martin knocked tentatively on the door, his knuckles scraping on its flaky surface. From inside a faint crunching noise approached. Moments later a figure, dressed head to toe in white pulled the obstinate door open by a few inches. 'Come in,' came the muffled voice. Martin followed dutifully, only then realising the source of the crunching as his foot sank into an unpleasant morass of pigeon shit. A quick glance revealed the muck lay inches deep, carpeting the floor and from it the heady smell of ammonia was eye-watering. Adjacent to the door he noticed the main staircase, which resembled a poorly constructed ski slope was similarly coated. His eyes returned to the figure in white. The man now lowered his mask which revealed a pleasant face, criss-crossed with red tram lines caused by its elastic grip. He shook Martin's hand tightly and introduced himself as Jonathon. Martin gripped his hand briefly detecting a faint Eastern European accent in the process. After a moment's hesitation Jonathon spoke.

'Mr. Stanhope said you would be by, and I have been instructed to let you have the free run of the place.' He gestured expansively before continuing. 'I hope you like pigeons,' he said, and chuckled to himself. Martin smiled and conceded it was a little worse than he had expected. 'Anyhow, this was the main banking hall,' said Jonathon leading his visitor inside.

The interior, much to Martins' delight was most certainly an undiscovered gem, even in its present state. Being one of the few undeveloped properties of that age left in the city, he felt privileged to discover its secrets. According to his research and before being used as a bank it had been a Georgian merchants house and further back, the site of Pitfodel's Lodging, a town house belonging to one of the Aberdeen's most prestigious families. Situated in the Castlegate, the area was steeped in dark history, witch burnings and executions having taken place on nearby Heading Hill. Strangely excited, Martin made a mental note to explore every nook and cranny and slinging his camera around his neck, followed his erstwhile host. It was a miracle he had secured the visit in the first place, and this was as close to thrill-seeking as he got given his natural passivity. Sad really, he thought, that a man of his age should get excited over an old building but still it was a harmless interest. It kept him out of trouble his wife would often say in moments of levity. And he agreed, for he had long forgotten what trouble meant. Perhaps it could be worse, he could have taken up bowling and he allowed himself an internal chuckle. Now standing in the hall they surveyed the accumulate pigeon corpses that littered the floor. 'Interesting,' Martin murmured. Jonathon frowned momentarily behind his mask, 'I suppose it is, but not much fun for me, I think.' Martin felt a tiny nip and slapped at the back of his neck, convinced a mite or something equally unpleasant had bitten him but observing his hand saw nothing. Jonathon laughed as if reading his mind, 'once you have been here a while you get used to it, but God knows I look forward to a shower in the evening.' And with that he led his guest across the room. Their feet crunched horribly across the debris and Martin to his horror noticed that everywhere skeletal remains protruded from the mire while nearby their livelier brethren flapped furiously against the grimy windows. There was something particularly hair-raising about birds flapping in an enclosed space, he surmised, his neck goosing at the thought. His train of thought was suddenly interrupted by Jonathon's muffled voice.

'It will cost 30K to clean, would you believe, and that's before they start any real work, and I have the dubious pleasure of doing that, I suspect I may be here for some months.' Martin, side stepping a randomly placed fire extinguisher noticed that on top of it sat a nest and he recoiled as its featherless occupants shrieked at his intrusion. 'Please mind your step,' said Jonathon, momentarily touching his arm, 'this place is full of surprises.' Martin mumbled his thanks, as the bug-eyed chicks continued to scold. The initial thrill he felt was rapidly dissipating and he soon found himself thinking that perhaps bowling would be better after all, at least the air would be fresher.

Jonathon halted suddenly and removing his mask turned to face Martin. 'The owner mentioned you like to photograph old buildings. Well, you should find plenty to interest you here. Follow me and I will give you the grand tour. Our feathered friends have only been here a short while, believe it or not......' Jonathon now headed upstairs and indicated that Martin should follow. Testing the first step with his foot it remained firm despite his reservations.

After the first flight Martin felt beads of sweat bloom and by the second was forced to lean against the jamb. The air was hot and cloying and it took some moments to catch his breath. At the far end of the room a door now lying on the floor, lay semi engulfed in filth. "The Raft of the Medusa," thought Martin in one of his rare moments of wit. Through the open doorway a panoramic view of twisted gables and weathered roofs lay perfectly framed. A light breeze from the nearby coast stirred the room and he was grateful for the relief it brought. He sucked the air in and filled his lungs. It felt good. Jonathon who had been standing behind tapped him on the shoulder and indicated the plasterwork. It was dilapidated and the scurrying of vermin indicated what lay behind the façade. 'Pest control will be in here in a week or so and then no more birdies.' He turned to Martin and to emphasise the point, drew his hand across his throat in a slitting motion. Martin felt queasy but Jonathon just smiled benignly 'Watch your step, now we go down,' and as an afterthought added, 'and if you must hold the railings remember do not to touch your mouth.' Jonathon chuckled softly enjoying the others discomfort.

Martin was hugely impressed by his joviality, and doubted he was being paid too generously for his efforts and so admired his fortitude. On finding themselves back on the ground floor his guide turned and bowed as if he had just delivered a well-received monologue upon the stage. 'The building is all yours,' quickly adding, 'but when finished, please let me know as I will be having lunch at some point and must secure the building.'

Martin nodded, 'Of course, I will come and find you, though it may be hard to get rid of me in a building as interesting as this.' He let out a weak laugh. It was high pitched and sounded false though his blushes were spared as Jonathon had already retreated accompanied by his tuneless whistling. Unsure where best to start and feeling like a child in a sweet shop, Martin pondered for a moment before plumping for the basement. The door lay opposite the main entrance and being ajar, revealed a set of granite steps that receded into the gloom. On entering he found the steps to be very worn and led down to a long earthen corridor. It was around 15 metres long and receded worryingly into the dark. Martin standing at the bottom, stood silently listening, while a distinct feeling of unease began to manifest itself. The basement looked no worse than above though admittedly there was much less light but that was not the issue, it just felt different. He glanced backwards at the shaft of light that illuminated the steps from above and felt marginally better and after giving himself a brief talking too, crept forward. On the left he passed three small gloomy chambers, containing nothing more than a few ancient wooden chests, the paper within those being pulped beyond recognition. He quickly regretted not packing a torch and so was forced to hold the flash down on his camera for illumination. The soft light revealed the same detritus as above. Ahead a bird could be heard flapping in the dark and he stopped momentarily, craning to hear its thrashings. It stopped and all was silent until a soft thud drew his attention. It was a not a particularly loud nor unusual sound but in the confines of the cellar it appeared ominous and so after a moments indecision he quickly retraced his steps. The staircase, with its comforting shaft of light now came into view and he strode purposefully towards it only slowing when convinced that something in the shadows beneath them moved. With his nerves jangled, a mild panic now overtook him and on hitting the first step lunged upwards before quickly reaching the sanctity of the sunlit hall. For the second time that day his breath came in shallow gasps. Once the thumping in his ears had subsided and the re-assuring sound of Jonathon shovelling merrily could be heard, he laughed and shook his head.

The next half hour, much to his relief was spent uneventfully exploring the lower rooms, the satisfying 'clicks' of his camera capturing another shot for posterity. Checking his phone he was pleased to note there was still plenty of time so headed upstairs. As he climbed, he made a mental note of what he had seen thus far. The attic which he had already visited was pretty spartan he reasoned, and so opted to leave it out concentrating instead on the floor below. There were at least three large rooms there if he remembered correctly, two having rather grand fireplaces. He also noticed that one had contained a few encrusted bottles, so perhaps a souvenir of the day was in order, though the image of his wife's disapproving countenance quickly dispelled the notion.

On reaching the spacious landing and with a choice of three rooms at his disposal he chose the immediate one on the left. On entering it appeared gloomier than he first remembered although he noted that the sun had dipped somewhat since then. Again, as in the basement, a faint apprehension had invaded his being and he stopped for a moment and listened. Outside the clouds which had temporarily blocked the sun had now moved on and a welcome mellow shaft shone through the large bay window. It was a beautiful room despite its condition and contained both a vast intricate ceiling rose and a large ornate fireplace. He strode towards the latter and with a quick scrape of his thumb, removed a flake of hellish brown paint, revealing its hidden charms. It was marble as he had suspected and on closer inspection a carved motif of what appeared to be 'Androcles and the Lion' could plainly be seen. He placed his hand upon the mantle, imagining its value and how it might look adorning his living room. It was quite something and he murmured softly in appreciation. It was then a dry rustling caused him to turn sharply. All was still though he continued to scrutinise the expanse like a shipwrecked sailor might scan the horizon for some moments. Eventually the need to draw breath snapped him from his torpor. There was something unnerving about the space, but he couldn't put his finger on it. A moment later he noticed that across the room sat a series of raised lumps. They were the ghastly remnants of old nests and would normally not have warranted much attention, but for one thing, he was convinced they had changed position. 'Good God, I'm getting nervous,' he thought and after several minutes of watchfulness admonished himself for his stupidity.

Shaking his head, he bent forward to adjust the setting on his camera before a faint sound had him snapping upright. It was the same as before, faint and stealthy but this time there was no mistaking its source as unaccountably one of the lumps now sat directly in front of him. An overpowering need to leave the room had now come upon him and on stepping forward felt the floor shift beneath his feet. With an audible gasp he quickly pulled his leg back, pressing himself against the cold surface of the wall behind him as a series of gentle undulations now rippled across the floor. To his relief the mass of decay writhing slowly mere inches from where he stood appeared unable to cross onto the bare boards which were now his precarious sanctuary. He continued to stare while the mesmeric qualities of its movement now held him in its thrall like a mouse before a snake. How long he had stood there he could not tell, but his feet remained immobile, locked within leaden boots. In desperation he willed them to move and automatically found himself edging to the left of the fireplace. Moving at an imperceptible pace his hands slowly worked the bare plaster as the distance between him and the door crept ever nearer. With his palms moistening at the prospect, every fibre of his being now willed him on. Within spitting distance of the door however his elation was short lived on accidentally kicking a chunk of fallen plaster. Rattling noisily across the boards the mass now alerted to his presence surged violently towards the spot where he cowered. With a barely suppressed cry he scrambled hastily back to the fireplace. As before he clung to its cold surface while ahead a deathly silence settled upon the room. Time ticked slowly and he wondered how long he had stood there. Afraid to reach for his phone he remained ignorant but either way he knew he would have to move sooner or later as a terrible numbness had now begun to spread across his stationary limbs.

In despair an image of Jonathon now formed in his mind. The picture of him merrily shovelling below almost made him laugh, though no sound came as his voice lay shrivelled and impotent within his throat. Minutes, possibly hours had now passed and the thing, whatever it was had now fallen silent. Martin knew that if he did not act soon his legs would buckle and acting on instinct picked up a chunk of plaster. Tossing it towards the right, the resulting noise caused the dormant entity to erupt into life. It was now or never and Martin with newfound agility leapt wildly to the left before skittering across the room. Clearing the doorway in a single bound he landed heavily his outstretched hands plunging deep into the morass.

Although momentarily ensnared he quickly pulled himself free, before a backward glance revealed further horror. The detritus which up till then had been content to remain shapeless had now formed what appeared to be a rudimentary body. How it achieved this, he could not tell but its arm-like appendages were now reaching clumsily towards him. Martin sprang upright and taking the stairs three at a time reached the ground floor, where he was horrified to find the front door firmly shut. Clawing impotently at its surface, it took some seconds before he noticed the scrap of paper pinned above his head. On it, a scribbled note brought a terrible realisation - "Sorry, I had to nip out for a bit. Nature calls. I will be back soon." Jonathon had decided to take an early lunch and in disbelief he tugged at the handle, but it was locked fast. Turning he clung to the door and listened. But the hammering in his ears made it impossible hear. A brief sob escaped his lips, and it was not until some minutes later that Martins breathing returned to normal. He listened intently but all was silent, the only movement being the dust motes pirouetting through the air. He dared hardly breath convinced the soft wheezing of his breath would attract whatever it was, but all remained silent, that is until a pigeon began to flutter in the banking hall. Its frenzied wings were now beating a tattoo against one of the rooms many windows and he found himself praying harder than he had ever done before. The question whether someone was listening or not was duly answered upon hearing a soft thud in the adjacent room. It was then he detected a sly rustling. Barely audible at first it soon grew in volume and a quick glance around the door jamb, revealed what he had dreaded most. It was the same figure he had narrowly avoided upstairs and like a magnet, it appeared to attract the detritus, carcasses and eggshell towards itself with each step. Groping blindly around the room, its hands now reached ahead of it. Though human in shape it had no head and its arms strained ahead seeking the spot where he cowered. To compound his horror an irresistible need to cough had now begun to manifest itself and he swallowed hard forcing it back inside where it lay dormant for several seconds. However, it would not be denied, and a dry hack escaped from behind his clamped hands. The shape ceased its fumbling and in response turned towards the sound. Realising his only means of salvation was now the cellar he plunged heedlessly down the steps and as before found himself in its gloomy confines. With the light from above momentarily extinguished Martin knew his pursuer had entered also and so ran. Passing the discarded chests his flight ended abruptly as his head met the unforgiving granite of the outer wall. Dazed, Martin sank to his knees and placing his hands to his ears whimpered as the sound of torturously slow steps approached.

When Jonathon returned around fifteen minutes later, he was perplexed to find no trace of his 'guest'. 'How ungrateful,' he thought, after scouring the property for ten minutes. 'He could have at least waited until I got back.' Clutched in his hand was a sheaf of photocopies and articles, which had intended to give to Martin containing notes on the area's history. Sitting down heavily he lit a cigarette before flicking through the bundle. 'Well, what am I supposed to do with these now?' He took another draw, before something caught his eye. On the second page was a description of Pitfodel's lodging, one of the city's most historic lost buildings which had once stood on the exact same spot where he now sat. He read on. Turning the page, a grainy image of the building caught his eye. The etching was dated 1650 and although the image was poor it was obvious that it had been a grand house. Surrounding the building was a substantial courtyard and grounds. Apparently the 'Scottish Maiden' had been kept there, a dubious honour indeed for the 'Maiden,' had not been a woman of flesh and blood, but the precursor to the Guillotine. On reaching the end of the passage he noticed that ironically the town executioner whose duties had included cleaning the blade of the machine had ended up as one of its customers. Jonathon smirked and placed the papers back inside the folder before lighting another cigarette. After some minutes he grabbed a nearby shovel and proceeded to scrape more debris from the encrusted floor.

A Dream Made Flesh

The venerable folklorist leant forward conspiratorially, the soft burr of his voice barely above a whisper. Alan leant forward craning to hear what was about to unfold. Stanley the elder of the two began. 'What I am about to tell you came to me in a dream and to this day I still wonder what lies beneath St Pauls'. Alan was all ears as the church to which Stanley referred to had captured his imagination for many years. This was in part due to its 'reputation.' Stanley continued, 'Its story is typical as after the congregation's numbers had dwindled, the area was earmarked for redevelopment and after the last ministers' illness it soon fell into disrepair. When the developers eventually moved in, it took just minutes to reduce it to rubble. Three years to build yet minutes to destroy. Aye it was a sad day indeed.' Stanley shook his head slowly.

'Sad indeed,' returned Alan now shuffling in his seat. In the silence that followed Alan quickly took in the room. The 'Blue Lamp,' Gallowgate's last surviving pub lay near empty. It was a chilly, Tuesday evening and the usual clientele mainly students from the nearby University were noticeable by their absence. Term time was over, and they had scuttled back to whence they came. Alan for one was glad as the noise level was subdued, all the better to hear the stories he had been promised. He raised his glass and sipped tentatively before his companion, teetotal and twenty years his senior continued. 'You know when they demolished the church, I really expected them to find something, and I am still convinced that what I dreamt was real, and that poor lassie was letting me know what had happened to her.' He cleared his throat and taking a sip of his rapidly cooling tea, paused for effect.

'What happened in your dream?' enquired Alan.

'It's such a shame' remarked the other deliberately avoiding the question, 'that a unique collection of buildings such as those were wiped out in the name of progress. Yes indeed, but as you can appreciate, we desperately need another shopping centre. Yes, perish the thought we should preserve our architectural gems at the expense of a cookie store.'

'Indeed,' the younger concurred. 'Strangely though I used to walk around that area at the time quite often but cannot for the life of me remember passing the church. Had I the interests I have today back then I daresay it would have never been away from the place, but please, back to your dream if you don't mind.' Stanley acquiesced before continuing.

'Well, the reason I am about to tell you this, is that I know where your interests lie and will take what I tell you seriously. I am psychic as you know and have spent many years investigating buildings that people claim are haunted, I can tell there and then on entering a building if it has an unusual atmosphere. I get an instantaneous sensation of either good or bad, I cannot describe it any more accurately than that and I have never been proven wrong yet. This is not a boast but a simple fact. Some call it a gift, if that is the case then it is one that I have never asked for. Being from a travelling background we as children were encouraged to look at things more deeply and to have pride in our ancient traditions. Most people call it superstition but that is our way, and nothing can change that. Anyhow, folk used to say things about St. Pauls that some might consider blasphemous being it was a place of worship, however I suspect even Gods' house can contain shadows. Anyway, it must have been around thirty years ago when I had my dream and it's stayed with me ever since.' Alan leaned forward slightly, his hand resting on his glass, before Stanley, clearing his throat, continued.

'The dream was so vivid and in it I felt as if my spirit had left my body and was floating through the streets like a wee light. I bobbed through the back streets of the city, drifting along roughly at the height of a lamp post. I remember clearly passing many windows and going down darkened streets and lanes. It was then that I noticed St. Pauls in the distance, its spire stark against the sky. Above it a few stars twinkled in the dark. As I approached, I began to feel myself lowering and soon I was through the old archway, you know, the one that used to stand on the Gallowgate?' Alan nodded. 'I then found myself going straight through its oak door and into the darkened church itself. I appeared to have no body yet was aware of sensations such as temperature and could clearly see my surroundings. Again, that pulling sensation drew me forward, this time towards the pulpit. It was then a sudden feeling of terrible dread came over me, a dread of what I might find there. This feeling increased but I was powerless to stop my progress and was now being drawn slowly towards a door which stood at the back of the church. As I got closer the feeling intensified and filled me with an exquisite horror, the like I have never felt since. I reached the door and was now compelled to go through it and then down the steps which led to the basement. I felt as if I had stepped back in time somehow, but how I knew this I can't explain. Once in the basement I noticed that a single candle burned on a nearby table and before it a man stood wiping his brow with the back of his hand. At his feet I could just make out the body of a red headed girl, although I couldn't see what she looked like. Her features you see, were obscured by the long red tresses which lay across them and for that I was grateful. There was a sizeable hole in the floor nearby and the man, sweaty and dishevelled, was gripping a shovel. An overpowering sense of evil emanated from him which was almost unbearable, but I felt trapped and unable to do anything other than watch. He turned slowly before facing me and I froze in horror. He grimaced and lifted another shovel of earth from the hole depositing it behind him onto the substantial mound already there. My eyes, having grown accustomed to the light, could now see him clearly and I took him to be around twenty-five years of age, handsome with thick dark hair. He was clean shaven and possessed the blackest eyes I had ever seen. He smiled to himself and again I recoiled as he faced me. Although I felt sure he could not see me, I knew he sensed me, and this made me terribly afraid. He looked toward his handiwork and smirked as the girl remained motionless. Who she was I do not know, but I instinctively knew she was Irish, and a poor servant lassie. With a sudden movement he bent forward, and seizing the corpse roughly began to drag her

31

towards the hole, at which point I woke. Let me tell you I was never more grateful.' A pregnant pause followed, and in those moments, Alan glanced across the room. In the interim it had gotten somewhat busier. A respectable smattering of customers now crowded round the defunct jukebox. Alan smirked, relishing the fact it hadn't worked in over ten years. At the bar the old guard now sat like three wise monkeys staring ahead while occasionally commenting on the state of the nation. Behind the bar, the owner Sandy smiled benignly, and Alan though tempted to order another for the moment waited. It wasn't often one got to hear stories like this first-hand and so he asked Stanley to continue. His soft couthy tones once again mesmerised his listener who remained content to nurse his dregs.

'Now as you know I have many friends and acquaintances and one of those is the Rev McGregor who has ministered at St Johns for as long as I can remember.'

'You mean the church on George Street?' asked Alan.

'Aye the very one. Well, I have known him for years and we are still good friends though for a while we lost contact, as happens. I doubt he would say this to many, but when I eventually caught up with him, I asked him about what he thought of St. Pauls. He became a wee bit vociferous on the subject and stated quite bluntly he considered it to be a gateway to hell.' Alans eyebrows rose slightly, a fact that did not go unnoticed. 'I know what you are thinking, why should a man of the cloth be bad mouthing a house of God and his near neighbour to boot? That was my reaction initially, but you will understand presently.' Stanley continued.

'Knowing that the building was on borrowed time I arranged to meet with the Rev. McGregor, and we poked around the outside of the church. It had lain empty for some time and its surrounding courtyard was overgrown and desolate. Once there we talked about this and that, church history, the development, local gossip. After some time, I became aware that there was something on his mind. At first, he was reticent to discuss the matter but on being pressed he seemed relieved to tell me. I had not seen him for quite some time having been away one of my lecture tours and so did not realise that since we had last met a new minister had taken up position in St. Pauls and subsequently left. During our conversation it became clear that McGregor had been quite close to him and as their friendship grew, he had become a regular visitor to the church. John Swinton was his name, and McGregor described him as being open, positive and fond of music, particularly jazz which my friend also liked. McGregor looked forward to their meetings though he could not shake off the odd feelings he had when visiting St. Pauls. He could never put his finger on it but would often find himself standing in its lofty interior gazing as if mesmerised but on leaving, he could never recall what had held his fascination. The church itself had no real architectural merit compared to other grander neighbours, a detailed window portraying the crucifixion was the undoubted highlight with a few pastoral scenes on either side for company. In truth apart from that the interior could have been best described as spartan. The decorative pulpit had been rescued from a much older church damaged during the war and so St Pauls' could not even claim that as its own. To be frank the interior was a little austere.

It was during these lost moments that the Rev. Swinton would inevitably appear and on shouting out a cheery hello, dragged McGregor from his torpor. McGregor liked his company and marvelled at how a man trapped in such gloomy surroundings could remain so jolly, but he did. He even wished at times a little of Johns' enthusiasm would rub off on him. Apart from their friendship, there were of course parish matters to catch up on though they seemed less onerous over a mug of tea. The Rev. Swinton was always glad of the company having lost his wife some years previously and he struck McGregor as a lonely man. This he surmised due to Swinton's habit of delaying his friend's departure always finding something to chat about upon leaving. McGregor of course didn't mind a bit and on visiting, absorbed a little of his friends' enthusiasm, which he lived off for the next few days.' Stanley paused, raised the cup to his lips and sipped slowly, before continuing.

'Swinton was by his own admission, a bit of loner. He had been devoted to his wife of ten years and when she passed suddenly, he was left rudderless. Soon after her death he requested to be moved as far away from the source of his grief as possible and subsequently found himself outside Aylesbury. He still couldn't settle however, and after a brief period asked again to be transferred. Some months later he found himself here in our beloved Granite City. One might have described it as a culture shock, but this is what his soul cried out for and was as far removed as possible from the surroundings that they had shared together both socially and geographically. His faith, he described, had been sorely tempted and in his darker moments had questioned his vocation but somehow the Lord had seen fit to grant him the strength to overcome. As an advocate of positivity, he soon riled his less gregarious acquaintances. This I knew because it was a topic of conversation that both men discussed at length. There was one thing however that nagged at Swinton and which he mentioned on occasion to McGregor, and that was a tangible feeling of being watched. This feeling did not manifest itself in his accommodation which sat adjacent to the main building for it was comfortable and light, but rather when he entered the church. It was a vague apprehension at first but over time its intensity grew. Strangely he found the feeling particularly potent, the nearer he got to the cellar door. A quick investigation would no doubt have proven his fears were unfounded, but a slight nervousness prevented him from doing so. That is until an opportunity presented itself soon upon the unexpected arrival of McGregor. Swinton of course was as always, delighted to have his company and after grabbing two torches from a nearby toolbox suggested they explore the cellar. They joked about what treasures they might find and there was a buzz of excitement about the proceedings. The door opened without protest revealing a large set of wooden steps which receded into the gloom. The steps lead to a spacious earthen cellar whose furthest recesses contained a vast array of chairs and folding tables. Dotted throughout lay random boxes of assorted bric-a-brac and they surmised if there was treasure to be found it was likely there. They were however a little disappointed on discovering that they contained nothing more than some particularly hideous ornaments. These included a headless statuette and some damaged figurines. Never fond of arachnids, their search disturbed a large spider, the sight of the plump creature eliciting a faint cry from McGregor. Swinton had laughed heartily and promised not to pry into any further boxes when in the company of McGregor again. They retraced their steps, noting some ancient gardening tools along the way. It was, they agreed a gloomy place, not made friendlier by the single bulb which hung from the ceiling.'

'Please continue,' prompted Alan, after Stanley halted momentarily.

Stanley surveyed the younger man's eager expression before sighing lightly. 'I am to a degree, paraphrasing of course but the bones of the story are factual, which can be corroborated. McGregor is also in possession of some notes, which he inherited after the 'incident, and to be frank, is still in two minds whether to have them shredded.'

'I promise it will be our secret,' said the younger of the two, 'now if you please.'

Stanley scrutinized the other for some moments and deciding him trustworthy continued. 'Weeks passed and having no need to venture back there, the cellar had all but been forgotten. It was true to say however that every time he passed the door, he felt a small frisson of apprehension. Why, he could not say and on mentioning it McGregor ever the pragmatist, laughed the notion off suggesting it was perhaps nerves. Sometime later he secured the help of one of the church volunteers, Mr. Craigton, and the pair set about stacking the furniture in a more appropriate location. It seemed a waste to leave such fine chairs to the dust and cobwebs and so they spent the morning carrying them upstairs. Once cleaned, they were placed in a narrow corridor on the left-hand side of the building, after which Mr Craigton made his excuses and left. It was then that apparently Swinton caught a movement from the corner of his eye near the lectern. On turning, he walked briskly towards it and momentarily caught a glimpse of a woman with long red hair who according to his testimony, disappeared through the cellar door. On reaching door he found it closed and pulling it open stared stupidly into the darkness for some moments before closing it securely. Retreating a little quicker than usual to the sanctuary of his office he then busied himself in parish matters. It was sometime later while poring over a recent circular that a loud knock reverberated through the building. He had jumped involuntarily, not expecting visitors, but was delighted to find it was McGregor at the door. Once inside the office Swinton presented him with a bundle of magazines which he had promised to give him for some time. The kettle was then boiled, and the offer of a cup soon followed.

McGregor delighted with his gift briefly scanned an article on the areas' history, while the tea was being poured. He was much amused to notice a headline, stating, "The Modern Parish Needs to Attract a Modern Audience," which he thought rather obvious. But before he could say anything his eyes were drawn momentarily to the opposite wall where a selection of portraits hung. The rogue's gallery he faced were all previous ministers of the church. It was strange, that even though he had visited on many occasions he had never really looked at them. "Thank God, my visage is a little more prepossessing or I would have a damn sight less parishioners," he had commented drily, as the faces, according to McGregor were in turn both terrifying and stern. He could imagine the service being accompanied by scaremongering of the worst variety. He got up and studied them more closely running his finger across the frames. They had at some time it appeared been framed *en masse* as they possessed similar dark wooden mouldings. Admittedly the most recent visages, for they were in order looked more appealing, but the further back they went less so. The facial hair in some were abundant and many sported walrus moustaches and mutton chops. One face however within that hirsute grouping, stood out. It was the face of a young man, handsome, dark haired and clean shaven. He had on further scrutiny the most alarmingly piercing eyes Swinton had ever seen and on viewing an involuntary shudder scuttled up his spine. The eyes he observed were near black and without appearing to be over dramatic he thought them malignant. There was the merest hint of a smile if you could call it that on his face which made him look strangely triumphant. 'Good God, I don't like the look of him at all,' he murmured, tapping the glass.

McGregor laughed, 'they are a little intimidating, aren't they? though I must admit I have never really paid much attention to them until now,' and with that continued to browse his magazine.

That night as Swinton lay in bed, he suddenly woke and detected the sound of someone softly singing. It was a lilting comforting voice and at first, he assumed he had left the radio on in his study. Fumbling to his left he clicked on the light and quickly scuttled to the study where he found the radio off. With a shrug he retreated to his bedroom and once back in his bed slowly warmed up again. Once asleep he succumbed to a dream. In it he found himself searching through the church, though for what remained unclear. I was told snippets of what he saw, sometime later.' Stanley continued.

'In his dream the church seemed cavernous, a hundred times greater than normal, the furthest recesses fading from sight. A cold and unforgiving breeze caressed his skin. It was the cold of a cemetery at night and with it, it carried a thousand horrors. Irrational terrors crowded his mind and he recoiled at the imagery. A face then appeared in his mind's eye; the face belonged to a dead girl whose features remained hidden behind a curtain of long red, wavy hair. He stood rooted and observed while an imperceptible breeze began to lift her vivid locks tantalisingly, threatening to expose her face. He desperately wanted to see but in truth he knew what lay beneath those red tresses. It was, he was convinced, an obscene travesty of a face as it had been sheared off. A sudden wind lifted the veil, and at that moment he shrieked with all his might praying the noise would rouse him from his slumber and it did. He sprang forward and found his hands planted on the table in the wardens' office. It was dark, and in the gloom the grim portraits of his predecessors stared blankly. All except one and his furtive glance revealed the malevolent features of the young man. Perhaps it was a trick of the light, but the smile appeared strangely broader than before. How he got back to his room that night remained a blur and as he had never walked in his sleep before the night's revelation disturbed him greatly. It was some time before he felt able to attend to church matters and in those ensuing days became moody and depressive. These were qualities new to him and it did not go unnoticed. On one occasion McGregor arrived unannounced with the hope of borrowing a table, which he had noticed in the cellar some weeks prior. At the request Swinton became somewhat agitated. "I'm afraid it is in the basement," he had said flatly. McGregor, momentarily taken aback, suggested he retrieve it himself, but his companion refused and stepped in front of him. "I would rather you didn't, we had a flood recently and the place is a bit of a shambles," he had said. Something in his tone suggested further discussion was not an option, so McGregor acquiesced.'

'In his defence and no doubt aware of his friends' incredulous looks, Swinton, promised to organise it. He appeared drawn and despite the cold a light sheen of perspiration lay on his brow. 'Have you time for tea?' asked Swinton, weakly after some moments.

'Well, I really should be getting back,' replied his companion.

'Please, do stay.' There was a tone of desperation in his voice. 'I would be glad to have a little company. It's been a very quiet week and what with the flood...' he indicated towards the door of the cellar.

'Very well, you've twisted my arm.' Said his friend, after a moments' contemplation.

'Splendid!' cried Swinton and with that slapped McGregor's back heartily with his open hand, an infectious smile breaking out on his face. 'Yes, lets drink to the success of our forthcoming fete.'

'Indeed but let us hope it's not a 'fete' worse than death,' chuckled the elder of the two, unable to resist the pun. With the kettle boiled the mood lightened considerably and the chat, irreverent as always, lasted near two hours before McGregor noticed the clock. 'Good grief, look at the time,' said the startled minister. 'I must dash, I promised to run an errand for someone,' and with that rose from his chair. At the doorstep, Swinton shook his friend's hand, possibly a little too firmly and held it for a few seconds. 'You know you can call me at any time,' said McGregor. Swinton looked slightly embarrassed and turned to escape his companion's unwavering gaze. After a moment he spoke.

'I hope you can forgive me about earlier; I have not been sleeping too well recently. I have also been asked to promote more community-based events and for the life of me, I'm struggling for ideas.'

'Yes, perhaps homemade jam and beetle drives aren't cutting edge enough for our young folk,' replied the elder.

Well, how about knitting then,' countered Swinton, and they both laughed. A moment later McGregor left and on turning to wave noticed his friend had already ducked inside. A shiver slid down his spine and thrusting his hands deep inside his pockets he headed for home under the rapidly darkening sky. Unknown to him it would be the last time McGregor would take tea with his friend under present circumstances.

Stanley cleared his throat, and sipping the now cold tea, pressed on. 'Unfortunately for Swinton, the events leading up to his mental collapse came quickly after. He was, I was told, plagued by a series of disturbing dreams which rattled his already frayed nerves further, and within a week was desperately ill. The doctors of course, relayed what had happened to the best of their knowledge, while various gossiping elements within the parish filled in the gaps. You will have to decide which is most palatable. Anyhow I have since met McGregor, and invariably the conversation has revolved around his now recuperating friend. It was fortunate that one of his parishioners had gone to pick up the furniture as requested or there might have been an entirely different outcome. On arrival and after receiving no answer he had let himself in and when inside discovered the door to the cellar was open. He called out and on hearing nothing was about to leave when the faint sound of sobbing reached his ears. In panic he ran to get help, being too afraid to investigate alone. McGregor quickly made his way to the church, and with the parishioner at his back crept downstairs. There they found a large hole which had been dug into the foundations. I know what you are thinking,' said Stanley, momentarily glancing towards the other, 'but it was empty.'

'It was there they found Swinton clinging to an ancient shovel, his hands bloody and raw. It was some minutes before they could persuade him to drop his burden and all the while he begged them to help, while tears tracked his grime encrusted face. McGregor now taking charge then sent the parishioner to phone the authorities while he remained, speaking to his friend in soothing tones. A short while later Swinton was led from the building like a child, mumbling 'she's in there you know,' the rest of his discourse remaining incoherent. The last thing they witnessed was his drawn face, staring out from the ambulance before the door slammed. As it transpired, it did not help that the parishioner was one of the world's greatest gossips and I'm afraid to say the news went quickly around the houses.'

'What happened afterwards?' asked Alan, after a moments silence. Stanley squirmed in his seat before continuing.

' I met McGregor sometime later and was pleased to hear that Swinton, under advice, had left his post. He now lives quietly with his sister in the country. His rehabilitation took many months and I doubt he will ever be the same, but nevertheless the outcome is better than expected. I have no idea if the doctors believed any of it or indeed if McGregor does. He has been very cagey on the subject but has told me as much as he knows. I suspect he felt better for unburdening himself and although I cannot verify every fact, this is what he told me.

Swinton, after saying goodbye to his friend, had spent the evening reading in his study, He was on the point of retiring to his living room when for some unexplained reason he decided to take one last look into the hall. It was there he saw the same young woman as before heading towards the basement and despite his fear decided to follow her.'

'What did she look like?' enquired Alan, his throat now strangely dry. Stanleys expression remained composed.

'She was described as having long red hair, though what she looked like I cannot say as her tresses obscured her face. She was wearing what he took to be servants' attire, the front of which was darkly stained.

Alan nodded slowly, before adding. 'Do you know what she wanted of him?'

'I do,' replied Stanley, 'she said she wanted him to help her dig. Make of that what you will but the result… well I have just told you.' Pre-empting his next question Stanley continued, 'of course the subsequent search revealed nothing. I heard he is doing well though,' added Stanley, after a brief pause.' His voice sounded almost cheerful, adding: 'McGregor keeps me up to speed on his progress and I am happy to report he is now enjoying long walks,' before adding, 'he has his sister's Lab for company you know. He certainly appears to have turned a corner. Of course, no one ever mentions St Pauls, so perhaps it was a mercy, it was demolished after all.'

The Other Side of the Door

Loitering outside the wash house of number 43 Sunnybank Road, Simon shuffled uneasily. For the past month or so he had consciously sought that decrepit wash house out. He could not explain why yet he was drawn to it inexorably and with great regularity. It floated seductively in his thoughts. Last thing at night it invaded his dreams, and in the morning, it greeted him continuing to drift in and out of his consciousness in the times between. His compulsion to see inside the wash house of number 43 had consumed him since the day he set eyes on it.

The door to the building in question hung loose from its hinges and so was permanently ajar. He had first noticed it some months previously while heading to work and had stopped briefly to observe its rustic charm. There was something mysterious and alluring about it, not necessarily the door itself, he argued, but what lay behind it. On passing several days later he was again stopped in his tracks at the foot of the stairs which led to the door. And so grew his obsession. The street on which it sat he concurred was

44

certainly not the quickest route to work, in fact that would
have been Erskine Street. The prettiest of all was without a
doubt Sunnybank Road to the right, but he chose the avenue
for no other reason than on it sat number 43. He remembered
frequenting the area as a child as his grandparent's had lived
nearby, and so knew the surrounding streets well. By the
1980s, what had made it unique, the old railway yard and
sidings had vanished. In its place now stood a retail park and
the ghastly smell of cheap burgers wafted from nearby vans
assailing his nostrils on passing. He loathed the sight of it and
what it stood for, so much so that every time he alighted from
the number 19 bus at the edge of the sprawling carpark, he
kept his head bowed to avoid its presence. Sometimes his
resolve faltered, and his furtive glances would elicit a barely
suppressed groan. On one such occasion a couple walking
past had given him a strange look, forcing him to quicken his
pace, until he had reached the nearby avenue.

On turning the corner, he was faced with a row of neat
granite houses. In front of each sat long narrow gardens
which led to the road. Some were well tended with grass,
manicured trees and bright flowers while others were not.
Perhaps he speculated they belonged to either the elderly or
infirm as they were weed strewn and wild. They punctuated
their more pleasing neighbours at regular intervals and in his
opinion let the side down somewhat. Some of the premises
however undoubtedly had younger tenants as witnessed by a
nearby gaggle of students' idling amongst the weeds. 'Lazy
bastards, there should be a law,' he fumed, stopping himself
before one of his internal rants began. After around two
hundred yards the style of the houses changed, the gardens
which had shrunk considerably now lay at the back between
neighbouring buildings. Separating each building lay large

well-worn steps and at the top the doors now faced one another across a plateau of concrete. Beyond this another set, much smaller, led down to the communal washhouses. He observed that from the street only the upper halves of those outhouses could be seen. Paying little attention at first, he glanced infrequently on passing but over time came to recognize his favourites. Most admittedly were past their prime, some missing doors, a few still in use. Others wore bright coats of fresh paint, but those were in the minority. It was the ones with 'character,' that he found most appealing and in their company one particularly dilapidated door stood out above the rest.

'Character,' now there was a word and though it covered a multitude of sins, in this instance it was warranted. On passing that first day his gaze was arrested by a particular fine specimen and on it he noted a brass number plate. Given its sheen it appeared slightly incongruous amongst the sea of flaking paint on which it sat. On viewing a strange sense of nostalgia washed over him and in the ensuing weeks had bathed in its warm glow numerous times. Why he liked this one door more than the others, he could not say. There were some far more pleasing to look at, take for example the door at 57, with its coat of pillar box red or the air raid shelter which stood next door. Both fine doors, and indeed fine structures but for some unfathomable reason it was number 43 that held his gaze. Perhaps it was the fact that the door was slightly ajar. Maybe it was the colour of the paint, pale blue, though he had never professed to liking the colour and in truth found it a little insipid. The reason remained a mystery, though its pull was inexorable. And so began, a slow-burn obsession with what lay inside. One quick look, what harm could it do? He often thought. He would then admonish himself for his stupidity. The internal conversation that followed would then invariably last till he left the area, only to return on his next jaunt.

Being naturally nervous, he had stopped himself just at the point of ascending the stairs on more than one occasion. What if he were caught, what would he say? He cringed at the thought, and recalled an incident when visiting his grandparents' tenement, some five years ago. In that moment his thoughts drifted back to their sunlit lobby where he had not stood since childhood, some forty years previously. Once there he recalled the pungent smell of Geraniums which had permeated the air while dust motes illuminated by the glare of summer twisted fantastically in the air. Outside through the coloured glass he observed a now plain lawn and to the left a neat row of outhouses. Back then a long vegetable plot had been in situ as had an iron rung ladder attached to the back wall, leading to a now removed railway track. He remembered it well, and how he collected worms from that long drill of earth. The worms he then placed in a large metal pale before presenting them to his mum. They had been a most unwelcome gift as she had recoiled in disgust. His mind travelled up the stairs trying to recall each piece of the puzzle, the living room with alcove, the scullery with the Belfast sink and Granny with a kindly given sweetie. He remembered her patience and he apologised internally as he was sure he had been a pain in the arse. A moment later light footfall sounded behind him, and he was swiftly dragged back to reality by the imperious tones, of an over-confident twenty something. 'Can I help you,' came the voice and he spun round to meet its' owner.

'Oh, hello, I hope you don't mind, but my Grandparents once lived here.' And as an afterthought added, 'I wanted to take a few photographs.' Like a child before a teacher, he felt his face redden.

His inquisitors face quickly softened, 'of course you can, I was just curious, I own the block you see.' Simon found himself at a loss for words and mustered a feeble smile in response.

Afterwards a sudden sting of bitterness pierced his heart. "Owner of the block, Christ almighty, she looks about twenty," he internalised and in the seconds that followed, he thought of his own precarious finances. In his mind she was only just out of nappies, it had to be a silver spoon job he concluded and feeling pissed off, stepped back into the street as his nostalgia trip came to juddering halt.

That night he had a terrible dream and woke with a start, convinced someone had been in his room he now lay staring ahead. Slowly his eyes grew accustomed to the dark but revealed nothing other than his furnishings. He moistened his lips and the images still fresh in his head, began to play over. He recalled that in the dream, for some unaccountable reason, he was lying outside number 43 in front of its worm-eaten door. It was bitterly cold. A strange compulsion now gripped him, and he felt compelled to see inside. He tugged vigorously on its rusty handle even though he Instinctively knew something unpleasant lay within. It was just as the door was about to give that a voice whispered in his ear and with it a ghastly image of something stick-like came to mind. It was some time before his heart rate slowed and even longer before he fell back into a fitful sleep.

On Thursday, he stayed home and slept well into the morning before rising around eleven. His mood somewhat soured by lack of sleep improved as the day went. As evening approached his anxiety once more grew but despite his trepidation, he enjoyed a peaceful night. On Friday while heading to work at the nearby community centre he returned to Sunnybank Road where he stood loitering outside number 43. While there he held his phone to his ear taking an imaginary call a habit acquired whilst trying to avoid unwanted conversations or divert suspicion. On the opposite side of the road a man washed his car, the water splashing noisily on the kerb, while behind him on a nearby wall a cat licked its arse. Still pressing the phone to his ear, he glanced over debating what to do. To his horror the car washer had simultaneously glanced back and Simon in a moment of paranoia, pretended to have a conversation. Certain that the car-washer remained suspicious Simon carried on the charade, smiling and mumbling unconvincingly. A furtive glance revealed the man had now ducked out of sight and was busily soaping the wheels. This was absurd, for six months, he had passed this building four times per week, before and after work. Damn it, he had even dreamt about it and in all this time had never seen a soul go in or out. It was obvious whoever resided there was at work and so to his surprise the decision was made and moments later found himself at the door.

On the top step a momentarily backward glance assured him that car wash man was unaware of his intentions. On reaching the wash house he noted that to the right lay a semi-manicured garden. It was all disappointingly normal and contained nothing more than an impressive array of blooms. A small trowel stood at attention in the nearest flower bed, testament to someone's recent toil while further along the rest of the border waited patiently for its manicure. In the middle lay the drying green peppered with daisies and wildflower and within that myriad of colour stood a solitary apple tree. It was beautifully serene. Despite this he was momentarily disappointed as to its ordinariness. A quick glance over the wall revealed similar neighbouring gardens all neatly partitioned by rubble walls. At the back door a rickety fence, the paint green and flaking ran the length of the garden while nearby a rusty hand mower stood. it was all normal, just a little unloved, but all normal. And with that his hand pushed the door to the wash house. Disappointingly, the ancient creak he had expected, was not forthcoming as it opened easily revealing an equally unloved interior. It was at first glance typical of its kind, a stone floor, once white plaster walls now grubby with age and in the far corner an old stone boiler. A chipped sink, half-filled with suicidal plaster from the ceiling above, sat beneath a window now obscured by a candyfloss coating of spider webs. Simon gasped, he hated spiders and to his mounting panic noticed they were everywhere. Admittedly most were dead, but their grotesquely hanging carcasses caused him to shudder. He rubbed his arm at their imaginary touch and stepped back deciding at that moment his curiosity had been satisfied and turned only to find the door now tightly shut. Against it, a homemade broomstick of sorts now lay propped, its spidery fingers filled him with distaste. Fashioned from dark wood it unaccountably filled him dread. Fumbling for the handle his grasp met thin air and to his horror noticed it now lay on the floor peaking out from beneath the tapering fingers of the broom. With barely any space between the door and jamb for purchase he crammed his fingertips through and received a splinter for his troubles. He pulled his hand back quickly, sucking the now throbbing digit. 'Damn it,' he cursed. Tugging with all his might the door began to wobble alarmingly and after a moment jerked open revealing the familiar steps. Outside he drank in the air, and it felt glorious. The splinter he decided could come out later despite its mindful throb, and as for the spiders, well they were more than welcome to the shed. He laughed and shaking his head admonished himself for his foolishness, the weight of expectation now lifted from his shoulder. After a few minutes and once suitably composed, he stepped onto the street. The cheerful sound of birdsong filled the air as before and across the street the car wash man, now busy with the wheel rims did not look up.

Around an hour later Simon stood in his kitchen, he felt agitated but could find no discernible reason for this. If anything, he should have felt relieved, proud even, and yet he felt no sense of achievement, no ticker tape parade or peace of mind. He then raided the fridge and ate till it hurt spending the next hour trying to read with the threat of acid reflux to keep him company. At 10.25 he put his book down for the fourth time and pulling on his jacket took a short walk round the block. Back home he opted for an early night, but sleep did not come easy. Around two hours later he at last succumbed but it was a restless sleep punctuated by an unpleasant dream. In it, he stood barefoot on the cold stone of the wash house. Above the sink the light from the window was much dimmer than before, its feeble rays barely illuminating the room. A tickling sensation caressed his skin which he itched at with nervous hands. Suddenly an urge to look outside came upon him and stepping forward, began rubbing the glass with his sleeve. The obstinate grime eventually gave way, revealing the garden now bathed in soft moonlight. It was a clear crisp night and the dark of tenement stood starkly against the deep blue of the sky. There was a pregnant stillness in the air. A feeling of anticipation. Suddenly at the base of the building where the shadows were at their densest an enormously tall figure slowly detached itself from the darkness. Simon held his breath and felt compelled to watch. The figure bent suddenly, its twig thin arms straining to pull a shapeless sack. The unpleasant dragging sound which accompanied its progress made him nauseous but try as he might he could not avert his gaze. Absorbed by the spectacle a feeling of dread slowly grew in his stomach. The figure now heading along the path which lay directly in front of the wash house halted abruptly and raised its head as if tasting the air. Its head now bobbling on a pencil thin neck and slowly turned, and Simon inhaled deeply as it now faced the window. The shape, perhaps realizing this appeared to languish in his discomfort, continuing to stand mere inches away. The air was still. Slowly, imperceptibly his eyes now grown accustomed to the dark was able to discern its features and it was not pretty. Wart-ridden and sallow, its eyes burned with inhuman malignancy. The face drew nearer, its breath now frosting the glass that separated them. It was at that moment that something grasped his shoulder from behind. With an ear-piercing shriek, the breath which had been denied for so long now found freedom. Leaping upwards in panic he found himself tangled within the confines of his quilt and was some minutes before his shaking hand found the courage to click on the bedside light. Delighted that it revealed nothing untoward he then repeated the process throughout the flat. Next came coffee and lots of it.

The next day and feeling somewhat worse for wear he took the practical step of avoiding the street altogether, opting for a slightly more circuitous route and on leaving work did the same. On the return journey he practically skipped home and felt lighter than he had in months and slowly over the ensuing weeks, the mania that had gripped him slowly dissipated. His health slowly improved and so on receiving an invite from one of his former students to visit, he thought nothing of it. Apparently having difficulty in choosing work for a forthcoming exhibition, his expertise had been called upon and Simon, flattered to be asked had of course agreed. As he had a relatively open week, he suggested they meet on Thursday afternoon. His enthusiasm however was dampened somewhat on receiving her address which was number 87 Sunnybank Road. Of course, having never been to her home before, why would he have known? She was local and had been for many years which she had mentioned on the odd occasion. That night a familiar feeling of anxiety now crept over him and for the rest of the next day an internal argument raged. He was being ridiculous, and he knew it and so after further debate formulated a plan to avoid passing 'the house.' If he approached from the right, he surmised, he could avoid passing number…… but he quickly blocked the image from his mind.

On Thursday, and with some trepidation, he arrived punctually at the agreed time and pressed the buzzer. It let out a feeble rasp and after receiving no answer he pressed with renewed vigour. After some moments the light shuffling of feet approached, before the chain rattled and the door slowly opened to reveal Margaret's kindly face. She appeared delighted to see him and seizing his arm he was led through to the dining room which served as her studio. While there he proffered a few pearls of wisdom in exchange for refreshments. Two hours later and with his belly groaning he at last dragged himself away. The sound of nearby rush hour traffic now filled the air and glancing at his phone he noticed it had gone 4.30. The bus would be here in ten minutes, and without thinking automatically took a left. Walking briskly, it wasn't till he was upon number 43 that he realized his error. His pace slowed and a near hysterical laugh now escaped his throat. It was insane, there was nothing in the least unusual about the building and yet there he was dawdling as he had done numerous times before. The inner dialogue continued as his legs automatically began to climb. He was now standing on the concrete plateau and on doing so stepped forward. The door still ajar, drew nearer and in another moment his hand raised and pressed against its flaking surface. It swung inwards, again revealing a silent world in which dust swirled fantastically and spiders lurked amongst the cobwebs. In the corner the boiler stood as it had done for the last hundred years, and on the door hung the ragged old fire beater. The broom with its crazy, witchy fingers, lay silently nearby. He stood and watched and listened. After some minutes, a vague movement drew him towards the window. Outside a group of men were gathered around a hessian sack which lay on the path. Three of them wore old fashioned raincoats, while the others, four in total, were in uniform. They were he surmised policemen and there was a look of revulsion written on their faces. The tallest of the three knelt and lifted the edge of the sack and in doing so revealed a small pale limb. One of the men gagged and on wandering off pressed a handkerchief to his mouth. Unable to move, Simon stood transfixed gripping the edge of the sink, his knuckles threatening to burst from his skin like overcooked sausages. The sky which had up till that moment been bright slowly darkened and the group now stationary took on the semblance of a sepia photograph before fading completely. It was then that Simon, wanted to run but he couldn't. Some unspeakable dread held him bound and moments later he knew why as a familiar spider-like figure crept from the shadows. He squirmed in terror, shrinking from the sight as a child would from a terrible dream. The nightmare, the one that had haunted him since childhood was now playing out before him. In it he stood in an old washhouse while outside stood a tall tenement much like the one he grew up in. The stone floor was icy cold to the touch and his head now lying upon it faced the door. Why he was lying there remained unanswered, but something was outside and trying to get in, something with stick thin feet which scratched the concrete with its every step. It was all coming back to him now. That exhilaration of terror he felt before waking. The screams that followed which would invariably drag him back to reality. The gentle comforting words of his mother. But this time there was nothing. Choking on a mouthful of dust, Simon scrambled frantically backwards as the broom or at least something like it now climbed down from the nail it had hung on. Raising its spindly arms in greeting it moved slowly towards him its dry rustling feet scraping the floor. In panic and with little option Simon found himself pressed into the space between the boiler and wall. An old fruit box splintered beneath his weight as he continued to burrow backwards shrinking from the touch of damp hessian. 'Ah there you are!' whispered a reedy voice close to his ear and with it thin witchy fingers, sharp and unforgiving began to prod his flesh, but by then he was beyond caring.

Three weeks later Janet found herself loitering outside the wash house on Sunnybank Road. She stared at it as if mesmerised. On the door on a brass number plate hung crookedly which read number 44. For the past month she had consciously sought it out, she could not understand why but she was drawn to it, the image floated seductively before her eyes, invaded her dreams, greeted her in the morning and drifted in and out of her consciousness during the day.

On a Ghost Tour

The Royal Mile or High Street as he preferred to call it, was busy as usual and Alan standing in a nearby doorway took a deep breath before joining his colleagues. There were three of them and each carried a large yellow umbrella with the words 'Free Tour' emblazoned across the vinyl. Despite his reticence he knew that being first on the rota for the 9.30 am shift there would be no escape and would have to run the tour no matter what. Jokingly referred to as the graveyard shift it was the arse- end shift which no one wanted to take. The history lovers of the day had now given way to the 'I'm not sure what to do crowd,' who despite their endless wanderings, felt obliged to shoe-horn another tour in before bedtime. The guides, he observed stood like predatory lions, a little to the right and warily clocked the gathering crowd. At first glance they appeared to be a rum bunch, a mixture of students, drunkards and a smattering of couples. After a few more moments the size of group had increased dramatically and with that he mentally began to prepare his opening speech. 'Anyone believe in ghosts? No!

well why are you on the tour then? He wished he had the balls to say the latter. The supervisor would then take a photograph of the assembled throng, the purpose of which was a head count for the owner, who would then bill the guide. It was a beautiful system…. especially for the owner.

The hands on the illuminated face of the nearby Tron Church clock now crawled interminably towards starting time and with each minute the crowd grew accordingly. It was painful to watch. A good proportion were young, obviously students, who would no doubt play the poverty card and as Alan milled amongst them, he strained to hear snatches of their conversations. It was shaping up to be the usual horror show. Continuing to survey the crowd, he drank in their features, listened to their stories and concluded that most, as assumed were just filling in time. Amongst those would invariably be several smartarses! All however had one thing in common and that was they had made their judgment upon the word 'free.' Most would of course know the concept of a 'free' tour but there was always a handful of miserable bastards, who took it literally. It was not helped by the fact that on the website any mention of tipping was buried deep within the dross.

With two minutes still to go four blank- faced, foreign students now sidled up and with that his heart sank still further. By experience he knew that certain countries did not have a robust tipping culture and concluded that if they made it to the end the best he could hope from them, would be the 'claw.' The 'claw' was a term used to describe the scenario wherein a clenched hand would slowly descend upon the outstretched palm of the guides before depositing a small amount of change. He had been given the 'claw' on numerous occasions and in doing so it had taken all his might not to return the bounty, with a sarcastic 'you keep it pal you must need it more than me.' Cursing inwardly, he was all too aware that winter was now fast approaching, and the prospect of a 'fat' Christmas appeared unlikely. A flash of anger coursed across his being, and he thought of his family. He felt guilty. He had been doing this for years now and felt at times like the proverbial hamster on the wheel.

Of course, he could be lucky and get a dream tour which occasionally happened and was the carrot that kept them all chained to this absurd way of life. Like playing slots it was at times soul destroying however if the jackpot came, it could mean perhaps £70, £90 or even more for one tour. Damn, he even knew of some guides who had reached the exalted heights of £200 for two hours work. Even he had neared this once and he literally and figuratively lived off it for days. Of course, with any gamble the banker usually comes out on top, and an image of his boss doing the backstroke through a sea of 'tenners' swiftly burst his bubble. It was then the supervisor approached and gave him the nod.

'Ok you can start now,' and with that, Alan delivered his welcoming speech. An amusing comment raised a chuckle or two and a few smiled but disappointingly the students at the back remained rigid. 'Who is here for the ghost tour in English?' Eighteen heads nodded. 'Can everyone understand me?' he further enquired. Again, they nodded. 'This is helpful because otherwise it might be a long tour for all of us.' A feeble witticism at the best of times but again it raised a few smiles, however the four wood - faces at the back remained impassive. He pressed on. 'As you know it's free to join this tour, there is no upfront cost to yourselves but as we are all self-employed guides and are not paid by the company, we are reliant on the generosity of those who join the tour'. He sucked in a lungful of air before continuing. ' And for that I will give you the best tour possible'. He then pressed home his advantage. 'At the end of the tour if you are unsure how much to give, hold a figure in your mind, wait 10 seconds at least, and then double it.' A polite ripple of laughter followed, though disappointingly the four at back remained stoic. 'Ah! the old pretending not to understand the language ruse.' thought Alan. Quickly asking where everyone was from, he eventually reached the four students who had arrived latterly. Hong Kong came the reply, on being asked.

'Well, welcome to you all. I'm from Scotland, now if you would like to follow me, we will begin the tour.' And with that the entourage snaked along the rapidly darkening street. Nearby a pre- pubescent minstrel had struck up a song and was wailing piteously about never finding love again, 'Jesus Christ, give it a chance pal,' thought Alan, concluding that he must have been all of eighteen. To make matters worse the troubadour sang in a strangled falsetto which made him sound as if his balls were being manhandled by a gorilla. The crooner whose bouffant hair now wobbled fantastically under his exertions, continued to spill his guts onto the street however Alan remained unmoved and ushered away his group as if avoiding a particularly gruesome sight.

Within a couple of hundred yards the caterwauling had faded which was just as well, as they had arrived at their first stop. Alan turned and faced the expectant crowd. 'Ladies and gentlemen, we are now standing in Parliament Square home to our original Scottish Parliament, has anyone visited our new parliament building by the way?' The question was met with a stony silence. 'Well, it looks like Ikea gone mad!' A couple guffawed loudly, which he found pleasing. His confidence boosted, he continued. 'Before we start, I'd like to ask, does anyone here believe in ghosts or the continuation of life after death?' around five hands crept upwards like slow growing vines. 'Are there any open-minded people amongst you?' he then barked. Again, a smattering of hands rose slowly. 'And lastly, please put your hands up if you don't believe in the supernatural.' One guy at the back who was tall and lanky, half raised his hand and grinned like a buffoon before nudging his partner. Alan inhaled deeply, he could tell instantly that he was a dick, perhaps even the king of dicks, and he disliked him intensely. How he longed to cut the fucker down to size, but at the last moment thought better of it, being potentially detrimental to his impending wealth. After clearing his throat he began.

'I know some of you might find this hard to swallow, but our first story concerns a young boy who was murdered and cannibalised and is based on real events.' The pun was lost on them, and an image of tumbleweed flashed through his mind. His darting eyes now alighted on a dumpy girl at the front who was aged around twenty-five and what little confidence he possessed slowly drained under her basilisk gaze. She appeared humourless and had already rolled her eyes quite openly. He looked away deciding to focus on the more pleasing visages sprinkled amongst the group. Once the story was complete, he then turned to face the Mercat Cross but before he could continue a rival company had stepped from the shadows. He recognised the guide instantly and though diminutive she possessed a voice which could shatter glass. She was Glaswegian and delivered her monologue in growling tones. She further ramped up her Scottish credentials by rolling her r's to an almost comic level. Her audience however seemed impressed and cowered before her aggressive monologue. Alan however was not impressed and being relatively soft spoken felt obliged to raise his voice accordingly. It was excruciating and for the next five minutes the guides battled head-to-head with Alan eventually throwing in the towel.

Now heading towards nearby Advocates Close, a fine mist had conveniently appeared. The group seemed suitably impressed and once in situ Alan launched into the grisly tale of Johnny one-arm. The story concerning landowner John Chiesley's torture and execution for the murder of a local judge was a typical dyed in the wool Edinburgh tale and Alan took great delight in recounting every gory detail. It was not a pleasant tale with the miscreant having his hand removed prior to execution. With the crowd now listening intently Alan continued. 'People claim that the discarded hand still haunts this area, pushing the unwary on the stairs of the nearby closes. Whether it's true or not I cannot say but a few years ago as we stood on this very spot, we heard a loud scream and on turning saw someone fall down this flight of stairs.' Alan observed their reaction before continuing. 'I was hugely disappointed however to discover that he had just been in the pub and was pissed!' A ripple of laughter rang out in the darkened lane and Alan smiled benignly, pleased that the crowd at last was warming to him.

'And now if you will follow me, we are going to talk about witchcraft.' And with that the group shuffled obligingly back up the stairs. The next two stops went without a hitch, they laughed at the right moments and were respectful during the more sombre. It was only on reaching stop five that he noticed that the 'four blocks' had slunk away. 'Sneaky bastards', he thought, though this was par for the course. His reverie however was interrupted by a drunk urinating noisily against the wall. He was a ghastly specimen and a few in the group sniggered, while several of the more delicate types looked mortified. 'Welcome to Scotland,' Alan shouted, attempting to deflect the horror and was rewarded with one of the biggest laughs yet. 'I think we should move on,' he suggested after the levity had subsided, and with that led them towards their final stop, Greyfriars cemetery.

Ten minutes later the group had now reached the end of the George 1V bridge where under instruction they halted outside Greyfriars Kirk. The idle chatter which had accompanied their journey for the last hour had now all but stopped and Alan smiled to himself. The area had that effect on people and the disquieting blackness that lay just beyond the gates, sat like a predatory beast. From the few half-heard conversations, he observed not all were desperate to go inside. Alan, taking that as his cue flicked on his torch, its welcome beam danced across the nearest headstones. He then cleared his throat and began. 'Ladies and gentlemen, our last stop this evening is the infamous Greyfriars Kirkyard considered by many to be one of Europe's most haunted cemeteries.' Several members of the group murmured in appreciation. 'Please follow me,' and with that he walked slowly towards the left-hand side of the church where they soon found themselves on a narrow path. Running adjacent to the darkened church it led into the furthest reaches of the Kirkyard. They crept onwards the beam from the torch alighting on each silent stone at their approach. Veering left the company now stood facing a row of silent burial chambers. There were around ten in total, and they had belonged to the wealthiest of the graveyard's inhabitants. Amid those stood a dome-shaped mausoleum, much larger than the rest and it was there Alan bade them stop. Raising his hands, he called for silence and the crowd did as they were asked.

He then began. 'Ladies and gentlemen, we are gathered at the last resting place of "Bloody George Mackenzie," a man responsible for the terrible fate that befell at least 1200 men. He is notorious in Scottish history, as being both cruel and sadistic and many believe him to be the unquiet spirit that haunts this graveyard. Why should he haunt here? And why would he want to harm those who enter his domain? There was silence, but not waiting for an answer he pressed on.

'Well, there are many theories, of course and there have been numerous eye-witness accounts from those who have experienced his wrath.' And with a last dig at the cynics, added, 'these witnesses, I can assure you are as rational as you or I.' The grinning buffoon at the back, and eye-rolling girl however still seemed unimpressed. He cleared his throat before continuing.

'On two occasions in recent years his mausoleum has been broken into and subsequently paranormal activity was noted to have taken place soon after. Is it just co-incidence, I will leave that for you to decide. In 2004, his last resting place was further desecrated. The group stood transfixed suggesting they were either impressed or had fallen asleep and being unable to see, Alan sincerely hoped it was the former. 'It's hard to believe but around ten years ago, two youths, both underage drinkers, were encouraged to break into this very tomb. Boys will be boys, and of course desperate to impress the young ladies in the group, they did, but it didn't end there……' The sentence was left momentarily hanging in the air, before he continued. 'The eldest you see, was in possession of a knife and decided in his wisdom to take a souvenir, McKenzie's head, which he cut from his body and took from this very vault!'

A few satisfying gasps rent the air and Alan sensing victory leant nearer and continued. 'After removing it he then kicked it around like a football, before being caught by a local guide. Multiple people witnessed this and of course they were arrested minutes later.' More incredulous gasps followed apart from the "grinning buffoon man" who sniggered, though that was to be expected. He continued: 'A passing tour company witnessed the whole shocking scene and I would suggest that they got their money's worth that night. After the subsequent court case, they were fined and given probation, not much of a punishment for such a terrible act, don't you think?' The group murmured in agreement.

'If you wish to find out more, go online and search for Greyfriars kirkyard desecration or words to that effect, and you will read the headlines that were written at the time. There is even a photograph of the lad responsible, and let me just say, he looked quite pleased with himself.' After a moments silence, Alan concluded. 'Well ladies and gentlemen that rather grim story brings us to the end of the tour. But before we part company are there any questions you would like to ask me? I will be more than happy to answer if I can.' The silence that followed, indicated a resounding no. Hoping his courteous manner might be looked upon favourably he then wished everyone a good evening.

True to form the group had now split into small mumbling pockets where the discreet rattling of small change filled the air. It wasn't an encouraging sound only made worse by the sibilant whispers that accompanied it. Alan continuing to observe, craned to decipher the near inaudible conversations as moth ridden wallets were trawled through. Depressingly, and within plain sight someone then tucked away a brown note in favour of coin. His heart sank even lower as in his peripheral vision he noticed several of his guests had already bolted. By God, they could move when they wanted to, he thought. 'Thank you for joining the tour,' he shouted into the darkness, his voice dripping with sarcasm. Cheapskate bastards, but that was to be expected. The remaining participants now filed past dutifully, and he shook hands on receiving each contribution. His palm like a bloodhound had now detected a twenty. This was rare beast indeed, and he shook the guest's hand enthusiastically. Next up a handful of sweaty change received a suitably limp handshake. It took some minutes before the group dispersed and afterwards, he stepped back into the shadows and quickly patted his pocket. It felt light and the following rummage confirmed his worst fears. Not a great bounty. Sighing he headed towards the gate, his mind now a jumble of thoughts. The wind was bitter, and he raised his collar to stave off its icy fingers. Maybe it was time to move on. How many years had been doing this? Too many, but for some reason he couldn't quite remember and feeling depressed thought of his wife and how much he cared for her. He really should head home. A distant sound then caught his attention and on turning noticed a large group had entered the Kirkyard. There were around twenty in total and like his group appeared to be a diverse lot. On passing he noticed that the guide was young and enthusiastic. She had brought them to a halt near the entrance and under instruction they had formed a tight circle. Alan, who, only moments ago had been on the point of leaving now hung back, observing. He really wanted to get going but felt strangely compelled to listen.

Once the group had settled, she cleared her throat and began. 'Welcome to Greyfriars cemetery, possibly one of the most haunted graveyards in the world and the last resting place of 'Bloody George Mackenzie, the Mackenzie Poltergeist.' Alan felt a strange drawing sensation course through his being and stepping from the shadows stood at the outer edge of the group. He felt a little self-conscious, convinced the guide would say something but she didn't and the group intent on her every word seemed equally pre-occupied. She continued.

'But before we head inside, I would like to tell you about another ghost that's alleged to haunt this area. Described by witnesses as being the spirit of a tall man, he has been seen at the entrance to this church on numerous occasions. What is most interesting though, is that it's been described as a contemporary haunting. The ghost you see, is thought to be that of a guide who was struck down by a car outside these very gates. As Alan listened, he felt decidedly queasy and attempted to cover his ears, but the sound of her voice now filling his head continued. 'It happened three years ago, apparently while he was leading a tour, now if you will come this way.' The group dutifully followed while snatches of conversation filled the air. At the back someone squealed having been pinched by their partner and the guide glanced back and smiled. Soon they were swallowed by the darkness. It was then Alan felt himself swoon.

Seconds later he found himself standing at the entrance to Stevenslaw Close. He felt cold and pulled his coat around him more tightly. Glancing upwards he noted that the time on the nearby Tron church was almost 9.30 and already a small gathering of tourists had assembled. They were a rum bunch, the usual mixture of students, couples and drunkards. At the front stood a sour faced dumpy girl. He didn't like the look of her and thought about his family and wished fervently he was back home.

The Bicycle

He came to regret many things on that fateful day, firstly his insistence on seeing the lovely Sarah, secondly taking the bend at a speed which one could only describe as perilous and thirdly seeking help at a nearby farm. Let me elaborate. Those who knew Dave, described him as being overly sensitive. Truth be told he was, he cried at the drop of hat, particularly when it involved the mistreatment of animals, he took umbrage at the merest perceived sleight, and when in love, took on the attributes of Galahad. Of course, a sensitive soul being told they are such is unlikely to engender a feeling of warm fuzziness and Dave was no exception. To make matters worse the lovely Sarah whom he adored, was an awful human being, but he was blind to her petty cruelties and had she murdered his family he would have likely forgiven her. The stinging jibes which followed their frequent arguments would invariably result in one or the other becoming petulant and withdrawn, as was the case in their most recent bout. The outcome was a temporary ceasefire in the battle of the hearts and as expected he had pined for days, that is until her signal flashed green for go. Typically, he had responded with indecent haste. Approximately 12 miles away in the neighboring village, lay his prize, and after three days of enforced celibacy he now drove like a man possessed. His head buzzed with thoughts of her wondrous visage, 'if only she was mute, she would be perfect,' he thought too preoccupied to notice a lone pheasant until it was too late.

Swerving wildly, the car stopped dead, axle deep in the verge. Inside the now stationary vehicle he began to pat himself wildly, convinced he had somehow sustained an injury, but he was unscathed. A glance in the mirror, to his relief revealed the pheasant to be in a similar condition. It screeched loudly and with an ungainly flutter leapt into a nearby field. He turned the key, and after some seconds it became apparent the car was going nowhere. Though no mechanic Dave felt it prudent to at least exit the vehicle for a cursory glance and in doing so the door met with some resistance. He strained further and after a moment succeeded in partially opening it. Once outside, he stood ankle deep in the soft loam surveying the damage. The car he surmised, in his own professional estimation appeared to be 'bollocked', a fact borne out by its refusal to start. Insult followed non-injury on discovering his battery power near flat lining and the practicalities of the situation was a six-mile hike in either direction. A quick glance at his phone confirmed the worst, he had roughly an hours' daylight left, so with little choice, he turned back towards home. Perhaps he could secure some help from one of the farms he noticed nearby. A phone call at the very least would guarantee him a lift if nothing else. 'Where were those damn cottages,' he mumbled, 'I could have sworn they were just round the bend.' But on turning he saw only trees. 'Perhaps it's after the next one,' he reasoned his pace now quickening, very much aware of the rapidly dipping sun. The birdsong that heralded dusk floated in the air. 'C'mon cars, where are you,' he groaned, but the road remained stubbornly empty. He cursed himself for his optimism, the image of a friendly driver delivering him like a parcel to Sarah whose sympathy would know no bounds, quickly evaporated. He stopped and listened. In the distance, the sound of an approaching car could be heard, and although still light, its headlights on full beam soon came into view. He partially raised his hand, attempting to keep his cool but the car and its occupants were already gone. 'Bastards!' he cursed, as the retreating vehicle shrank from view, its lights now extinguished as it took the bend.

He trudged on his mood lightening as the promised farmhouse at last came into view. Breaking into a trot the thought of romance once again surfaced temporarily, until his foot snagged against something on the verge. He glanced down grimacing in disgust at the sight of the near skeletal hare which lay contorted on the grass. As a teenager, he had stumbled across a similar sight and the memory still haunted him. The head had been eye-less and had grinned up at him from the dirt, its teeth exposed in a rictus grin. On inspection its awful skeletal legs had retained fur bootees and his skin had crawled at the sight, much like now. Walking on quickly, he continued to glance back, convinced that the carcass would rise and follow him, or even worse touch him. It was madness of course so he pressed on and within another minute stood at the foot of the darkening path.

The farmhouse now directly in front, looked grey and forlorn and after navigating the weed strewn path, he stood before the door. Disappointingly it looked derelict and a series of sharp knocks on the door, did nothing but dislodge a few of the flakes which still clung tenaciously to the wood. He stepped back and looking upwards noticed two of the windows were missing panes of glass. A quick glance revealed the steadings on either side were equally dismal, one hosting an ancient mound of manure. It did not look promising as the various rusted implements testified but unwilling to give up just yet, he took a right and continued his search. Thoughts of finding a back door however, proved fruitless as he was soon met by a mass of impenetrable brambles. Retracing his steps, he again hammered loudly, but received no response. It was then he noticed that to the left of the door a bicycle lay propped against the wall. It was a real boneshaker, its buckled front wheel held prisoner by the fronds that encircled it. He stepped forward and placing his hand on the saddle withdrew it quickly. It felt clammy, unclean even. Further scrutiny revealed a light green mold peppering the leather, and he wiped his hands against his jeans in disgust. Glancing upwards, something white had appeared momentarily in the top window before quickly vanishing. 'So, there is someone in,' he mumbled, before stepping back for a better view. It was a decision he regretted instantly as his foot sank into a deceptively deep puddle. 'I just bloody bought those,' he hissed as the cold muddy water encased his trainer. Stepping back from the puddle he continued to watch the window, but whoever it was had gone. Convinced that something had retreated rapidly from his view, he remained fixated for some minutes before continuing to explore.

The light now slowly fading, was not enough to induce panic but certainly caused him mild consternation and so picking up his pace, he went left. On reaching the back of the building he found a long, narrow strip of grass surrounded by a tangle of trees and shrubs. Like the property, it was unloved and wholly depressing. It lay bathed in shadow and in the air a heady smell of damp and rotten vegetation hung. The shadows which appeared deeper than those at the front did little to dispel his growing unease. However, it had at some point been manicured and despite the overgrown rose bushes, it was relatively clear. A few thorny hands attempted to impede his progress but being resilient, and with newfound hope, he located the back door. On reaching the door he found it ominously ajar and after receiving no reply to a volley of loud raps, took a deep breath and squeezed through the crack. Inside, the kitchen lay still, and he half expected the owner to come lurching out of the gloom but there was only silence. 'Hello,' he called, his voice echoing horribly, and a mild panic fluttered at his breast at the thought of someone replying. But all remained silent. It was, as he had first thought, deserted. A strange melancholy hung in the air as he observed the pathetic remnants of the late owners' life strewn haphazardly around. On leaving the kitchen he then entered the hall. There were four rooms running off it. To the right there was a dining room while opposite what he assumed would have been the living room. It was difficult to tell in the fading light, the furniture in both were so completely blanketed by detritus as to make it impossible to tell. He entered the first and found it contained a large leaded fireplace which would at one point have brought life to the room. Above the fireplace a series of pictures hung. He drew his finger through the dust which revealed a kindly face, he tentatively wiped the grime away to get better look. After a moments' rubbing the image became clearer and was that of a middle-aged woman, smiling and confident. The clothes suggested the 1950s, he replaced it carefully and retraced his steps to the hall. Now facing the main door, the monumental pile of mail which lay underneath the letterbox drew his attention. Bending, he scooped an envelope from the top. It was dated 24th August 2009, eleven years ago, give or take. It was addressed to a Mr. John Thrower. Casting it aside he picked up a generous bundle and began flicking through them slowly, John Thrower, John Trower, Mr. J. Thrower, Ryan Thrower. Well, if nothing else, he knew who the last tenant had been and with that replaced the letters.

Why had he left, he pondered but his curiosity was quickly dispelled at the sound of someone moving softly in the room he had just vacated. He stood listening as the blood slowly hammered in his ears. The noise, and it had been a noise, came again. Cautiously he re-entered the dining room and noticed for the first time the terrible odor which permeated the room. Summoning up what little courage he possessed he attempted to call 'hello,' but to his shame his voice weak and high sounded childlike. There was no reply, but the smell, God the smell! It reminded him of something, something he couldn't quite place, but it brought with it a wave of nausea. And then he remembered. It had been at his auntie and uncles' cottage. It had lain just off the main Stonehaven Road, a coastal village in the northeast. The building, nestled in a small dip and surrounded by tall mature trees, had been a source of adventure as a kid and he had loved being there. These infrequent visits were regarded as something special and so the memories were easily recalled. After tea, he had been sent out to play no doubt to give the assembled adults a break and had found himself rooting about the outbuildings. Inside the nearest he had found a dead and bloated cat though whose cat it was remained a mystery. His uncle, alerted by his cries, had dutifully shoveled it into a bag before disposing off it discreetly, pressing a small coin into his hand as a means of compensation. Dave's mood had brightened considerably and after wiping away his tears with a grubby sleeve had flown off to play. He wrinkled his nose in disgust at the memory but was soon drawn back to reality by a faint noise in the hallway. It had sounded like a soft tread and so creeping forward he listened while his head now floating like a nervous balloon, drifted cautiously around the doorframe. To his relief the hallway lay empty but now the same faint creak sounded upstairs. His neck snapped upwards in panic and again he listened but could hear nothing. With his nerves now stretched to breaking point he admitted defeat and quickly squeezed himself out of the back door. Outside he breathed deeply and with discretion being the better part of valor, headed towards the road. Walking with renewed vigor, he noted the remaining light now lay perilously close to the horizon and the sky had become home to a multitude of twinkling stars.

It was then he noticed the man, a short distance away at the entrance of the larger of the two steadings. The figure, who had not noticed him, appeared to be looking at something within the building and after a few moments slowly walked from sight. 'Hey! excuse me,' Dave shouted, happier his voice now carried some authority. 'Excuse me,' he repeated, now splashing across the mud in pursuit, but on entering he found nothing. The intense feeling of dread which followed then sent him scurrying from the farm and within seconds he had reached the lane. Half an hour earlier it had appeared almost welcoming, but now in the near dark, a new world had revealed itself. This was a world where grass and leaves conspired to trip, and horrors hidden within the undergrowth waited seize the unwary. It was a world of decay, and he wanted no part of it and so ran.

The grey band of the road was now in view and a mild elation urged him on. Slowing momentarily to catch his breath, it was then he realised he was not alone. Behind him the creaking sound of a rusty unused machine was getting closer, and a frantic backward glance revealed the bone shaker. Now upright, it bore down on him, its pedals producing an awful screech as its speed increased. An abject whinny erupted from his throat at the sight, and he went sprawling headlong though his fear hoisted him immediately upwards. The pitch of the rapidly gaining bike had now become an ear-piercing shriek and he fell heavily smashing his knees upon the rough path. Despite the jarring pain he rose once more and in the remaining light saw that atop the machine sat a thin cadaverous figure, with high cheek bones and empty sockets like that of the hare. Its clothes appeared tattered and were horribly stained while upon its head a few strands of hair flapped behind it as it gained upon him. A rushing sound then engulfed him and with a cry of despair he flung himself headlong into the mire as the bike, now losing momentum wobbled past his inert body.

After some minutes David rose, his heart still pummeling in his chest, and glancing fearfully at the bicycle which now lay on its side. It was with some trepidation he approached it but to his relief the bike remained stationary. Limping the last remaining yards, his feet at last struck the blessed tarmac. It was only then he allowed a brief sob to escape his lips as the dull aches which encased his body began to manifest, but he staggered on, the farm quickly receding with each step. Ten minutes later with his breathing now returning to an acceptable level he saw the first twinkling lights of civilization. It was a cottage, one which he had passed earlier and on reaching the door tapped gingerly. Some moments later he was greeted by the surprised owner who took the sight of his mud splattered visitor well. Ushering him inside, a stiff drink was then placed in Dave's hand which he finished in one gulp. The owner, a local farmer, instantly poured him another and with that the spirit worked its magic. A warm fire now crept slowly to his belly and though keen to hear his story the farmer waited patiently until his guest felt ready. Soon after, and with a faltering voice, he recounted his experience and only upon finishing did the farmer break his silence.

'Are you sure, it's the farm just a mile or so back?' he asked, pouring his trembling visitor another drink.

'Yes, I'm sure, it had two steadings one on either side and the farmhouse in the middle, there's a line of trees directly behind it.'

The farmer, now playing with his empty glass, replied. 'I know the one. I used to visit there now and again though the owner John was a bit of a recluse. He was nice man but distant particularly after the death of his son.' The farmer continued with a faraway look in his eyes. 'Shame really, a nice young lad, about your age, died in an accident, some idiot driver speeding, knocked him off his bicycle. An old bone shaker it was, used to sit out the front door, said he couldn't bring himself to get rid of it. He would have been better off without it. In the end his grief ate him up, it was a terrible shame. The place has been derelict since he passed away, must be over ten years now.' Dave's eyes moistened and he took a hard swig of his drink. Strangely he hadn't thought of Sarah for some time.

The Trunk

On viewing the house for the first time, her disappointment was apparent. Michael on the other hand insisted it was a grower. The house, their house, stood on a cliff and on their arrival the rhythmic lash of the tide below provided an unrelenting soundtrack to the proceedings. The pastoral landscape of England, which they had left mere hours ago suddenly seemed a lifetime away and Janice felt sorry for herself. Michael typically already seeing the positives, seemed unaware. If he was aware of his wives' unhappiness it never showed. Seeing the house just once himself, he had drawn a veil over its less attractive qualities, the details of which he and Janice were now obliged to discover. The house itself, somewhat dilapidated, could best be described as a project.

On entering it was, as he remembered, a little grander than its neighbours and consisted of three large ground floor rooms. Off the connecting hall lay an ancient kitchen and utility room. The kitchen was in poor shape, having never been touched in decades and Janice, on seeing it for the first time baulked at the idea of preparing food there. A lone woodlouse ambled across the blackened linoleum adding insult to injury. Outside the kitchen sat a broad staircase which led to three further rooms. All were spacious. Further investigation also revealed a dust strewn attic whose initial discovery had conjured up images of antiques and rare books. Unfortunately, the excitement had withered quickly as it was found to be empty bar a brown leather trunk covered in a prodigious layer of dust. The lack of electric lighting and the miniscule windows only added to its ambience. It was a cheerless place. The trunk, however, begged to be opened, though the hope of finding something of value evaporated when it was found to contain nothing more than a horrible looking stain across the base. It was a rusty brown colour and Janice felt herself shudder involuntarily. And so, with the treasure hunt over the rest of the afternoon was spent moving boxes. At around 8.30 they sat amongst the debris and drank wine, allowing its warmth to rob them of motivation. It was most definitely a work in progress, thought Janice.

Some days later, with the boxes lying empty and crushed inside the garage, their contents now adorned the shelves of their new home. Janice wandered from room to room feeling lost hoping the familiarity of those objects would elevate her mood, but they didn't. The circumstances of their sudden move now flooded her thoughts. Michael had been given the raise he had always strived for but at what cost? With most of the week spent travelling around the country it would leave him with little time to deal with the multitude of tasks that needed addressing. Frustration hung in the air and the isolation crushed her. After lunch she headed for the cliffs basking in the elements. The fresh air was certainly bracing, but after five minutes it felt as if she had been sandblasted.

The dryness of her skin now added to her growing list of misery. Little wonder there was such a proliferation of ruddy cheeks amongst the locals, she thought.

Some weeks later, Michael on one of his rare weekends at home, had at last managed to prune the garden into some semblance of order and to Janice's joy an antique bird bath had been discovered hidden amongst the brambles. But it still wasn't home. Perhaps it was the fact she had given up a lucrative career to follow him that still irked her? Or was it because he was wholly unaware of her needs? It was probably both, and she felt a sting of resentment. Despite keeping busy she could not shake the slow depression that had begun to infiltrate her mind and slowly retreated into herself. She stopped taking calls, now resentful of her friend's assumed perfect lives, and in an exercise in self-punishment cut ties. If they somehow got through the barricade, she was icy and abrupt, and all the while Michael remained unaware.

Her sleep pattern became disturbed, giving her further opportunity to wallow in self-pity, and it was on one of those nights, she woke to an inner nagging. It was not a quiet slow awakening, but rather a sudden jump-start and for a while lay there obliged to stare at the ceiling. After some minutes her breathing slowly returned to normal. A dry cough now rattled in her throat and reaching for a nearby glass, found it empty. Loathe to leave the sanctity of her bed she clung to the hope her cough would ease but it persisted and without hope of relief she eventually rose. The house was silent, bathed in moonlight and the kitchen with its ancient surfaces appeared clean and spotless in its silvery glow. Turning on the tap she stood at the sink when an awful sensation scuttled down her arms. It felt like being trapped in another's body as a strange numbness now engulfed her. It was the strangest feeling, completely alien, and her movements became slow and un-coordinated. She felt her hands tapering uselessly ahead of her from shoulders that were broad and ungainly. Filling the glass, she lifted it slowly and drew it towards her mouth. It felt heavy and she gulped a mouthful before setting it down clumsily. Her hands felt almost arthritic and appeared near useless and she found herself pressing them together with mounting panic. It was then that someone touched her. She spun round violently to find no one there. 'Nerves!' she said aloud and took the stairs at an indecently fast pace. Once inside the bedroom she switched on the light and stood listening, her ear to the door, but all was quiet. Her hands felt normal and holding them in front of her she drank in their familiar creases and veins. 'Pins and needles,' she murmured but part of her remained unconvinced. Once under the covers sleep eventually claimed her.

Spring became summer and in the interim Janice had gotten to know some of the villagers, at least on nodding terms. These included an elderly couple from across the road, the Maitland's. They made small talk for an hour and promptly vanished. Afterwards she wondered if it had only been an excuse for them to look around the place but soon chastised herself for being so mean spirited. There was, as she soon realised a village mentality to the populace. Friendly chats became inquisitions, and she was reticent to divulge too much. Perhaps people considered her strange, the thought had occurred to her. Michael on the other hand had no such concerns, having been a near lodger in his own home since his arrival, he had barely spoken to anyone. This suited him, having never been the most gregarious of individuals he remained preoccupied with his work. On occasion, when the subject of his wife's loneliness was brought up it was instantly put down to change, lack of hobbies or anything else he could pluck from the air. The unpalatable truth, however, was that he was emotionally unable to support anyone other than himself, a fact which Janice had been prepared to overlook at first. Now of course, his self-absorption had come to roost. 'If he wants to be a bloody hermit, let him get on with it,' she had hissed, more than once.

Towards the end of Summer and in one of her brief forays to the village she visited the post office. There she got chatting to the postmistress, Margaret. They had of course already exchanged pleasantries but as there was no one around a conversation developed. Janice, a good judge of character, was in doubt as to the woman's gossiping nature but reasoned without 'ammunition,' she could do no harm. The postmistress slumped over a crossword had glanced up on her entering but remained impassive. Janice, purchasing some stamps, had then instigated the conversation. Like a coiled spring the elderly worker leapt on the opportunity, no doubt hoping to wring as much information from the newcomer as possible. Janice soon, finding herself on the receiving end of a mild inquisition skillfully guided the conversation to the subject of local history. The postmistress somewhat disappointed at having been on the brink of prizing opening the marital closet, conceded defeat and began a discourse on all things local. What skeletons that lay therein she reasoned, would for now remain hidden. Janice pressed home her advantage and Margaret, flattered that someone should seek her expertise, soon forgot her disappointment. Their house, according to her newfound confidant, was apparently an architectural gem built some 200 years previously. Owned by a succession of notable individuals, these had included two teachers, a ships' captain and a minister, whose church still stood some two streets back. Fascinating as it was, a surreptitious glance at the clock revealed her impending lunch hour. She had been standing for over an hour as her protesting stomach testified. She thanked Margaret and with the promise of a return visit, left, whilst the bell jangled behind her. On reaching home she ravenously devoured a bowl of soup, mopping up the remnants with hunks of crusty bread. Pushing the plate away, she breathed heavily before grabbing a nearby pen and paper and for the next ten minutes wrote furiously trying to recall as much information as possible.

Excited to impart her newfound knowledge she quickly prepared some food in advance of Michaels return. At the table that evening however, and much to her annoyance, his reaction was decidedly underwhelming. He seemed disinterested, chewing thoughtfully with just the occasional nod. The remainder of the meal passed in near silence and once the table was cleared, they retired to the living room. A cheery fire crackled in the hearth and room temperature quickly rose sending them into a near catatonic state. Janice topped up her glass, and the evening drifted comfortably towards bedtime.

It had now been over four months since the move and despite her initial protestations Janice had grown accustomed to village life, spending a couple of afternoons a week in the nearby town. Attempting to cultivate hobbies, she read voraciously, took up baking, something she had up till then avoided. The cakes, at least those she couldn't eat, were given to the gulls, their noisy appreciation making her smile. Soon after a cat began to make its presence felt too. It was, she assumed an elusive beast as on feeling its soft fur brush against her legs she had reached down to stroke it on more than one occasion, only for her hand to meet thin air. She kept busy while Michael, driving to God knows where, would disappear for days. The weeks slowly passed and soon the chill winds of late Autumn whipped around their home. The sun now appeared less frequently and when it did it neglected to bring warmth. Janice, now spending more time indoors, looked from the window content not to have to deal with the garden. The lawn had given up growing some weeks back and the plants which populated the borders had begun to turn a deep russet whilst others shrank back into the soil to avoid the scolding wind. On Friday evening the familiar sight of Michael's car arrived at around 7.30. It was already getting dark and after a cursory hug they now sat at the table sipping their drinks. She felt happier that he was home and held his hand as if to emphasize the point.

That night they retired early though Michael's snoring made a mockery of Janice's insomnia. It was near one in the morning before she eventually succumbed to sleep but the nagging dream which followed kept her close to wakefulness. In it, someone was creeping through the house searching in the kitchen below. The drawer opened slowly and cautiously. It was a secretive sound, but it was the creak of light footfall on the stairs that eventually plucked her from sleep. Confused for some moments she sat upright. Her throat was dry, and she glanced longingly at the nearby empty glass on the bedside table. A soft thud from the attic drew her eyes upward. Now the sound repeated except it was nearer the door. Whatever it was had moved. She hissed at Michael, but he remained oblivious until a firm hand dragged him from his slumber. After a few moments' befuddlement he too lay listening. The movement so soft and hesitant was hard to place and it was with some reluctance they left the warmth of the bed and ascended the stairs. Stopping outside the attic door they listened. Something was inside the room. With a silent nod Michael opened the door slowly. The attic now lay silent, and the probing beam of his torch revealed nothing. Somewhat relieved, he remarked. 'Nothing here.'

Janice, insisting on further inspection, seized the torch from her reluctant husband. Now casting grotesque shadows across the timber, she continued to play the light into every nook and cranny, but it revealed nothing more animate than dust. As a final measure, and in no way reassured, Janice then lifted the lid of the trunk, the sole inhabitant of the attic. The same foul smell as before wafted out and Michael stepping back wrinkled his nose in disgust. It was an odd sickly smell, like decay, and it tickled unpleasantly at their nostrils. 'I told you; it was nothing,' he said, glancing towards Janice with a look of condescension. Realizing his insensitivity, he touched her arm and gently guided her towards the steps. It was, 'probably just the wind,' he said to placate her.

For the next three nights all remained quiet but on the fourth the same light tread was heard above. Michael once again rudely dragged awake arose as before. Silently creeping from the room, they again pushed open the door to reveal nothing. Afterwards they retreated to the kitchen for some tea where they were surprised to find a multitude of dusty prints across the floor. They were paw prints from a cat and a large one at that, however the preceding search revealed nothing more than a large hole beneath the sink near the pipe feed. 'So that's where the little bastard is getting in,' crowed Michael, looking vaguely relieved. 'I told you there would be a logical explanation.' He patted her arm. Janice hated it when he patronized her. 'I think we should try and get some sleep,' he mumbled and being in no mood for conversation she agreed. It was now 2.40 am, and back in bed she stared fixedly at the ceiling for the next hour, unable to sleep. Michaels' accompanying snores served only to remind her how different they had become.

The next day they kept themselves busy, neither felt sociable, and Janice, opting for a walk, had left early. In the distance thunderous clouds loomed and within ten minutes the first drops had begun to fall but it passed quickly and within minutes the gulls were out again. She closed her eyes basking in the warmth of the sun and slowly felt better. It was a glorious feeling. After some minutes she continued her walk and soon another mile had been eaten until at last she halted out of necessity rather than exhaustion. Ahead and to the south, a dark and foreboding sky indicated an approaching deluge and so after a moments' indecision, she retraced her steps. The clouds now following kept a respectful distance until reaching the garden wall. It was there they relinquished their watery cargo, the warm raindrops splattering noisily. Pushing the gate open, she quickly entered the house. Inside, while the kettle boiled, she pressed her nose against the grimy pane. The garden had all but vanished under the force of the downpour. Washing her hands at the sink, she retrieved a dishcloth from a nearby drawer before slowly and methodically drying them. It was then she began turning the cloth back and forth like dough before realizing that the hands she was so meticulously drying were not her own. They were care worn and broad not delicate and thin. A sharp tingling sensation coursed through them and with mounting panic she placed them on the work surface before her, where they lay useless. The fingers thicker and shorter slowly flexed and lifting them to her face she allowed them to explore her features like a sculptor would clay. The face was also not her own, the nose being broader and the mouth wider and with that sudden realization she let out a cry. Michael, in the next room, was with her in seconds and with his touch and reassurance she regained her composure. He looked worried, almost laughably so, but she later assured him it was nothing. Her mind, she reasoned, was playing tricks on her. That night she dreamt again. It was a vivid dream and in it she found herself on the landing. Once there she looked over the banister and saw to her alarm the figure of a man slowly ascending the stairs. He was dressed completely in black. His hair, also dark, was curled and rested on broad shoulders. Gripping the rail, she continued to watch his progress as his hand thin and hairy slid up the rail ahead of him. At the turn of the step his face was revealed but on suddenly waking she could not recall what he looked like.

The next day Michael left for work and after a brief hug and weak smile he slammed the car door shut. He would be back by Wednesday, or at least that's what he said. From the garden, she watched the car retreat up the hill. A near neighbour waved across briefly and Janice for the sake of politeness flashed a brief smile before heading inside. It was getting colder, and she quickly pulled on an extra jumper. At around mid-morning she played the radio for a while but switched it off when the presenters' banality got too much. A gaggle, of sycophants could be heard laughing at DJ's every word, 'toadying bastards,' she thought, 'play some bloody music,' but he didn't, preferring the sound of his own voice. Next came a book, but the words remained a jumble, and after re-reading the same paragraph twice it was consigned to the "for later pile." Next came the paint, which thankfully proved to be more of a meditative experience and with each brush stroke, her uneasiness lessened. Being a work in progress it was also eventually discarded. The kettle went on again. Later, she drank tea on the step and listened to the waves as the sun in its zenith provided scant heat. She glanced at the clock. A horrible anticipation was in the air. She returned to her painting, but the light had faded and so found it impossible to continue. Afterwards, she settled for a drama on TV. but finding the plot to labyrinthian for her mood she changed channels, once, twice or more but on finding nothing that appealed, switched it off. The silence was now crushing.

Outside a black sheet now hung against the panes and a quick glance at her phone indicated the time. It was still only mid evening, but the nagging feeling of unease which had haunted her all day was now thick in the air. To drown the silence, she increased the volume of the T.V, but an irrational fear of it drowning out 'other' noises forced her to reduce it. As the evening progressed, she became convinced she was not alone and eventually reached for the off button before spending half an hour just listening. Angry at her own irrationality she then poured a drink first fiery gulp causing her to wince. A second and third followed and at last the tension eased so when bedtime arrived it was with slightly less trepidation that she mounted the stairs. The fourth drink had been the clincher. The bedroom was noticeably colder than the living room and so on clicking on the side light, she wasted no time in climbing into bed. The sheets felt damp at first, but after five minutes a soft warmth encased her. Visualizing her room as a little bubble of light floating safe and secure in the dark, she soon succumbed to sleep.

In the morning she woke late after having a better sleep than she had in weeks. Perhaps alcohol was the answer she reasoned. After a quick breakfast a visit to the library followed. On arriving she spoke briefly to the librarian who seemed helpful and threatened to secure some archival material regarding the house. Spending a pleasant afternoon there, she browsed and took notes before returning at around 4.30pm. Thirty minutes later the phone rang. It was Michael, he had been given some good news, regarding his work. A new employee would now be sharing the load as of next week, which for him would mean less travel. However, there was a change of plan as regards his return and he would now be home in two days' time instead. Janice sighed but kept her voice upbeat. Afterwards she consigned the half-cooked meal she had been preparing to the bin, preferring the slow anesthesia of a rapidly depleting bottle. Three drinks in and Janice turned the heating up as the chill of evening began to bite. Outside a fine mist whispered over the grass and from the living room she could see it curl and pulsate in the breeze. She poured another and slumped before the T.V drawing a blanket across her shoulders. On the screen, Pippa and Henry were extolling the virtues of owning a second home in France. They looked smug, their cut glass voices drifting from the screen assailed her ears and with that she could feel her temper rise before venting her fury at the screen. "Oh, how lovely, fuck the locals why don't you, lets price them out of the market, pricks probably voted to get out of Europe, happy to bloody live there though! European only when it suits." She suddenly realized her folly and smirked, perhaps drink five should have stayed in the bottle?

Sometime later she woke with a start. Voices from the T.V still burbled but now the room had gone cold, and the lights were off, though she swore they had been on. Pippa and Henry had long gone to bed and now an overweight man played darts. She pressed the remote to off. The dull persistent ache of a hangover was now apparent and although reticent to leave the room she quickly dashed upstairs. She flicked the switch, only then remembering the bulb had needed changing and so made a grab for the vanity light above the sink. It flared into life momentarily revealing the face of a woman maybe fifty or sixty of age, careworn and sallow. The woman's mouth moved soundlessly trying to articulate, while her hand clutched at her throat. Janice found herself mimicking the action and backed away in fright. Seconds later she woke with a start and found herself still on the settee, entangled in the throw.

The short call she received around breakfast time did not improve her mood. It was Michael, he would be back later than planned, something about work, another opportunity, this would be the last time. "Yes, yes, that's fine, are you sure, so you're going to be back then? Ok, I see, good luck then, see you soon." The words tumbled robotically from her mouth. The voice on the other end sounded distant and she detected hurt but under the circumstances she could live with the guilt.

At around ten she was alerted by the persistent ringing of her phone and scurried to find it. Frustratingly it rang off before she could locate it, however, she discovered a voicemail had been left from the local librarian. It was a pleasant surprise as their previous conversation had garnered results, the librarian's message alluding to the fact she had dredged up some information regarding the property. Once in the car, the drive to Peterhead took around seven minutes and after negotiating some notoriously difficult parking arrangements found herself outside the library. The building typical of its age was austere though beautifully designed. Two half-moon windows lay on either side of the main door and the tiles at the entrance remained as bright as the day they were set. Inside to the left was the children's section while adult lending and reference shared the rest. Upstairs were the archival rooms, and it was to this area she headed. On arrival she was greeted by the librarian who looked pretty much as a librarian should, somewhat meek in her demeanor and plainly dressed. According to her badge she was called Fiona and appeared delighted to have been given a task. She smiled broadly indicating that Janice should be seated before disappearing into a room behind the front desk. Once seated Janice surveyed the room. In the corner sat two men, whether they knew each other or not was a matter of conjecture for neither spoke preferring to scan the headlines of their respective newspapers. In the furthest corner and to the left a younger man, a student she guessed, sat at a laptop his ears encased in oversize headphones. Elsewhere a few casual browsers pondered at the shelves. She also detected the faint sound of a child crying in the distance which suggested the kids' section had at least one unwilling visitor. A moment later the office door swung open on its well-oiled hinges and the smiling librarian re-appeared with a large bundle under her arm. 'Rocksley house? yes I know the building, it's the one near the lighthouse, and what views!'

'Yes, they're very dramatic,' Janice said smiling in return.

The Librarian, appearing satisfied with the response continued, 'I have some photocopies which may be of interest to you which you are most welcome to look at. We also have a small online archive. The villages history is my passion, so I put together a bundle after my colleague mentioned your interest. My grandmother was born there you see, I suspect that's why I'm so fascinated,' and with that passed across the bundle. Janice smiled and looked around for a seat plumping for one near the window. For the next two hours, she browsed the contents. The articles covered everything from the opening of the primary school, teachers' past and present, fishing, and more fishing. Grainy images of the village and census records breathed life into its inhabitants and clippings told of landmark events. Most of the content of course was banal, arguments over building rights, congregation numbers decreasing, the inquest into the death of Captain McGuire. Her eyebrows suddenly rose. 'Fiona, excuse me,' she called over, 'but have you heard anything about this?'

Fiona taking the paper, read quietly. 'The inquest into the death Captain McGuire is to take place....' but the article was faded and poorly copied. 'Would you like to hear about it?' she enquired, perhaps a little too enthusiastically. 'I remember hearing about this from my grandmother, she liked to tell a good story.' Janice nodded.

Fiona beamed, 'well, one of the village's most prominent citizens was accused of poisoning his wife. My grandmother told me she was found dead in the attic, and her husband, Captain McGuire took his life while awaiting trial, in Aberdeen.'

'That's horrible,' said Janice feeling suddenly queasy, 'do you know why he did it? '

The librarian, lent forward conspiratorially, 'he accused the poor woman of having an affair, unfounded of course, but that's what he believed. My grandmother knew all about it of course being local.'

Janice felt a little lightheaded but went on. 'I know, I sound morbid, but can you tell me where I could find more information about this? I'm just being curious,' she added apologetically.

'Well, I would be happy to make enquiries on your behalf. I know the central records are kept in our main branch, and it's possible they may have better preserved documents, I can certainly ask, but it may take a few days for them to get back to me.'

'That would be very much appreciated, just when you can,' replied Janice. They thanked each other profusely, one for retrieving the information, the other for being saved from terminal boredom and with that she left.

It was on the return journey that she made a mental note to ask, no, tell Michael they would be seeking a new home! No amount of money would induce her to stay longer than necessary. They had savings and so homelessness was not an issue. The internal conversation rumbled on in the preceding miles only ceasing when she stood outside the gate. Once inside she attacked the list, she had mentally prepared earlier, spending the next three hours in glorious mind-numbing domesticity. A hot bath followed in which she floated in near relaxation, barely glancing towards the ceiling. Once downstairs, she sipped tea, her face pressed to the glass once more. A quick glance at the mantel confirmed it was almost nine o clock, soon the street- lights would spring into life. Across the road, Mrs. Davies dog could be seen urinating against her sun bench. Normally she would have smiled, but she felt anxious. After some pacing, she switched on every light within the room and turning the T.V on sat down heavily. Michael would be back tomorrow, and she was resolute.

She switched on the television but the preppy young historian emoting on the 'War of the Roses,' failed to ignite her interest. No room for dusty old farts these days Janice mused. Sometime later she jolted awake. The hands on the clock had reached eleven and it took a few moments to gather her wits. Thankfully the historian had now become history and it was a politician who now stared from the screen nodding sympathetically while deflecting questions with the ease of a tennis player. She felt agitated and so when the interviewer began worrying him like a terrier would a rat she felt oddly satisfied. He was merciless and kept at him and she smiled at his discomfort. And so, for the next while one program slipped into another. After some time, despite wishing to remain awake, her head began to dip. It was a losing battle and the more she tried to concentrate on the television the more she found herself nodding. Sleep now pulled at her eyelids and soon after she slipped from consciousness. She slept fitfully before waking abruptly and found herself on the landing. How she got there, she had no idea but there she was gripping the banister with both hands. They were clumsy hands, the same as before and with mounting panic she allowed her eyes to travel down the length of her body. What the hell was she wearing? She didn't even have a dress but was encased to her ankles in a ghastly light blue gown. It felt rough against her skin and around her waist a white apron, tied in a crude knot completed the ensemble. Her hands, lacking sensation, numbly began touching her hair which was much shorter than she

95

remembered. A strange rasping sound escaped her throat. It was then she became aware of someone moving slowly through the house.

Listening intently, she detected the scrape of a chair being slowly dragged across linoleum soon followed by the soft tread of feet. The steps appeared unsteady and became louder as they entered the downstairs hall. After a moment's hesitation the steps now slowly upwards, the stairs creaking in protest at their approach. The steps were now accompanied by the sound of harsh breathing, it was an unhealthy sound the product of too much tobacco washed down with alcohol. Now compelled to watch the figures approach Janice's heart hammered deafeningly in her chest. When the figure was halfway up the stairs it stopped and slowly raised its head. Though hard to discern in the half-light he looked to be around middle-aged. The face slack and ill-shaven was near expressionless apart from the eyes which burned with silent rage. They were spiteful eyes, vicious, callous, fueled by disappointment and alcohol. A foul smell which she likened to mildew hung in the air only added to his malevolence. Taking two more steps he slowly raised his arm and with a trembling hand pointed accusingly in Janice's direction. Janice stepped back, shrinking into the shadows to avoid his awful gaze and in doing so found her hand grasping the handle of the door which led to the attic. Fumbling desperately the door opened with a click but before she could enter the sound of his footsteps had broken into a run. Moments later she woke up with a scream.

How long she'd been asleep for she could not tell but on waking quickly became aware of a terrible sensation of cramp. It was pitch black and on her first attempt to straighten her legs found it impossible. Confused, her knees were somehow now directly in front of her face. With mounting panic, she again tried to rise but only succeeded in dashing her head against what appeared to be a wooden surface. The sound reverberated in her ears as did the scream of agony which followed. Again, she tried to rise only to be met with the same unyielding surface. It was then she realized she was inside the trunk. Sobbing, she quickly became aware of the sickly smell of decay. In the confines of the trunk, it was unbearable, and she gagged as it crept up her nostrils. Within a further minute what little air there was had become fetid and her breath now labored in shallow bursts. But it was when the agonizing cramps set in that her cries of desperation became truly deafening.

In the front garden a police officer scratched his chin slowly with his pen and on entering the door took the chair opposite to the one in which Michael sat. He rubbed his head slowly, methodically, allowing his fingers to roam across his scalp as if trying to massage some understanding into it. 'So, Michael, I hope you don't mind me, calling you by your first name?' asked the officer. Michael glanced towards the ceiling where the sound of people in white suits could be heard moving around the property before returning his gaze to the floor. 'No, no, that's fine.'

'I understand how much of a shock this must be for you, Michael, but I just want to get an idea of how this might have happened. I'm afraid, I must ask these questions.' He paused before continuing. 'How long had it been since you last saw your ex-wife?

Michael continued to rub his head, 'It would have been around six months ago, just after our divorce came through, before she moved.' His eyes moistened before he continued. 'I have no idea, why she wanted to come to this Godforsaken place, in the first place? I told her it wasn't a good idea, but she wouldn't listen. She was still angry I suppose, but I never harmed her, ever, or cheated on her, despite what she thought...' his voice began to quaver. The officer nodded.

'How long do you think she had been in there for?' asked Michael, after some moments.

The officer took a deep breath, 'Well as you know it took several days to locate you, and prior to that we think, though I can't verify this at present, she had been gone for several weeks. A neighbour phoned when she discovered the door was unlocked, and without going into too much detail she realized immediately that something was wrong. What's puzzling though, is why she was in that trunk in the first place? The catch must have slipped of course, but why on earth would she have climbed inside?

'I really couldn't say, I'm at a loss!' said Michael, continuing to gaze at the floor.

One Gelder Bothy Night

A welcoming light twinkled from the single window of the Gelder bothy as Alistair approached. It had just gone seven and the pale winters' day had given over to night some three hours ago. A helpful moon had kept him company since then, kindly illuminating the snowy landscape. The surroundings hills, now encased in a white mantle, had made the last two hours walking difficult and with each step his boots crunched through its icy crust. He was chilled to the bone, so it was with some relief that his destination lay just ahead. For the last two miles his mind had been occupied with thoughts of a roaring fire and so on arrival was somewhat disappointed to notice a set of vague prints leading towards the door. Company was the last thing on his mind however it was brutally cold and the surrounding hills, barren and uninviting stretched unbroken in all directions. It was an unforgiving landscape and on nights such as these any shelter was preferable to another ten miles of blundering. Besides, the village had limited accommodation or so he had been told and with the recent snowfall it would be besieged with visitors. So, with his icy breath now billowing ahead of him he passed the straggle of trees which surrounded the building and upon reaching the door stamped his feet once before pushing the latch inwards. Once inside a surprised, bearded face greeted him. The man who he judged at first glance to be around forty practically leapt from his seat by the fire and he found himself apologizing for the intrusion. 'Well, hello! I didn't expect to see anyone on a night like this,' said the stranger, with a broad smile.

'Me too,' replied Alistair, and realizing he sounded a little accusatory, smiled and pushed a sodden hand toward his companion. 'I'm Alistair, and I really should listen to weather reports more closely in future,' he added. The bearded stranger continued to smile and receiving his hand shook it firmly.

'I'm Steve, and ditto,' and with the ice broken, at least on the inside, they each took a seat by the fire. Mercifully, someone with great foresight left these,' said Steve, after a few moments, indicating the split logs and kindling, which lay to the left of the hearth. Alistair clapped his hands together with glee, remembering numerous occasions when he had sat before a black and lifeless hearth. It must have been a quiet season, he surmised. After a few moments he removed his jacket and hanging it over a nearby chair, dragged it nearer the fire where faint steam rose from the garment. Both men stared into the flames and in no time the chill that had plagued him for most of the day had gone. Steve, turning back from the fire, then retrieved his rucksack and after a moments' rummaging produced a silver flask. 'Would you care to join me in a small libation?'

'Why I would be absolutely delighted,' returned Alistair. And they both chuckled.

Steve poured out two generous measures and after a short toast, the warming glow crept towards their grateful stomachs. The conversation now easier, ebbed and flowed and both men finding common ground chatted for some time about their occupations. As it transpired, both worked at various times within the third sector and although Steve was a little younger, they both shared mutual acquaintances. Another log soon found its way onto the fire and fresh flames toasted them gently. 'Well, I for one am delighted, I don't think I have ever had such a comfortable evening here before,' remarked Steve.

'Oh, so you've been here before?' asked the elder of the two.

'Once or twice,' said Steve, his face now orange in the glow of the fire. 'The first time was around five years ago, and I joined some friends merely out of curiosity, because of its reputation. I wasn't much of a hillwalker but tagged along as an excuse to see the place. Since then, of course, I have gotten the bug and try to hike as often as possible.'

The other nodded. 'I feel the same and without sounding too dramatic, I only feel alive when I am out in the hills. There's something magical about it, getting lost in ones' thoughts, everyday worries vanishing and the greatest of joys found in simplicity. A well-earned rest with a crust of bread can seem like a banquet. But what did you mean, about its reputation?'

Steve continued: 'well back then one of my main interests was researching Scottish folk tales, legends and the supernatural. I collected as many stories from the region as I could find, which I found fascinating. Of course, being an armchair adventurer, I never bothered to visit most of the locations, that was until my visit to the Gelder. It is reputed to be haunted and this is of course what prompted me to visit.'

'Did you experience anything?' asked Alistair after some moments.

'Nothing,' came the reply, 'though I retain a healthy respect for the possibility.'

'It's certainly the kind of place where one's imagination could wander,' remarked Alistair, before continuing. 'I must though admit I'm fairly impressed with it, I've certainly stayed in a lot worse, though maybe the whisky is helping.' Raising their glasses, they toasted their good fortune until a sudden noise outside ended their revelry. Someone was outside and after a few moments of fumbling the door flew inwards. A blast of icy air fanned the flames briefly as an imposing figure entered. Bracing himself against the mounting storm, he pushed the door shut with a mighty crack before turning to address the company.

'Gentlemen, excuse me for the dramatic entrance,' he said in a soft voice that belied his physicality. Both men, startled, drank in the sight of the new arrival. He was tall, well over 6ft, and on his craggy jowls sat a weeks' growth of grey hair. His eyes though pale and watery, were keen and alert as he surveyed the tableaux before him. The silence broke as the same mellifluous tones assailed their ears. 'I hope you don't mind sharing your oasis with a fellow weary traveler?' he enquired after a moment's silence.

Both men remained transfixed until Steve, first to gain his composure spoke. 'Of course, there is always room at chez Gelder,' and smiled displaying the same warmth afforded to Alistair a mere hour ago. The stranger did not return the smile but thanked them nonetheless for their kindness before slumping heavily into the chair nearest the fire. 'My god its cold!' he murmured, rubbing his hands alarmingly near the flames. Steve poured him a drink and set it at his feet while the stranger continued to heat himself. Alistair, feeling a tinge of annoyance at the intrusion, put his good manners to the fore and reached across offering his hand, but the stranger who appeared preoccupied, did not acknowledge. Instead, he sat back and stared at the flames with pale unfocused eyes, before announcing.

'I am thankful I found you, I have been here before and found no one. It can be a depressing place if alone.'

'I for one am very glad of the company,' said Alistair, suddenly feeling sorry for their cold visitor, and they raised their mugs in mock salute. The stranger who seemed unaware of their welcome continued to stare ahead, as the flames crackled in the hearth.

After an uncomfortable silence, Steve then suggested building the fire a little higher, and Alistair in agreement seized an armful of kindling before placing them on the hearth. 'That's more like it,' he said with a look of satisfaction. He then turned to the stranger, 'I was just telling my friend that I have been here before. I believe it has a bit of a reputation among climbers. Have you heard anything of it yourself?' The stranger remained momentarily impassive, before he spoke.

103

'Indeed, I have. I am well acquainted with the stories relating to this area. But of course, people claim many wild areas to be the haunt of bogles and spirits.' And as an afterthought he added, 'as Scots such thoughts are deep within our psyche I believe, but the Gelder, well now that is a different matter entirely.' He spoke slowly as if savoring the words, before continuing. 'I have heard many things of course but it has never stopped me from coming here. How about you gentlemen, do you believe in the existence of ghosts? I don't mean wailing grey ladies, or the headless animated corpse of some poor soul, doomed to walk a castle battlement, but something real, that has perhaps in some way attempted to prove its' existence to you.' His voice trailed away, before continuing to stare as before. Steve breaking the silence, countered.

'Well, I for one, believe that there are forces in this world that we do not understand, and though no expert, I do find the concept fascinating.'

Alistair, normally reticent, and due in part to the drink, began to speak. 'I have never had the pleasure of an experience myself, but I know someone who did and in fact I was unwittingly present at its coda.'

'I would love to hear of it,' said the new arrival, flatly, continuing to stare into the flames, 'and I must say, I am hugely impressed that neither of you flew from the conversation as many would. I'm usually wary of encouraging such talk with strangers lest they think I'm a madman,' he chuckled softly, 'but I can assure you, you need not worry on that account.' And with that placed both hands upon his knees.

Alistair felt a little sheepish at being the center of attention, but on seeing the intent on his companions faces, began. 'My interest at the time, around 10 years ago, was taking architectural photographs of buildings that were earmarked for demolition. I had a deep dislike of the planning department in my hometown who appeared hell bent on continuing their scorched earth policy of, "if it's auld ding it doon", a term which is self-explanatory. Of course, they all thought themselves experts, and the viewpoint of the average citizen was duly ignored due to their lack of expertise. Having letters after one's name, it would seem, entitles the holder to make blanket decisions for the rest of the populace. Though to be fair the current crop of jokers is only part of a lineage consistent in their ineptitude. In a nutshell, extremely poor choices were and are still being made in preserving our built heritage.'

'Hear, Hear,' Interrupted Steve, but a sideways glance from the stranger quickly dulled his enthusiasm.

Alistair cleared his throat before continuing. 'For months, if time allowed, I patrolled the streets photographing the constant changes. During this time the old bus station, Victorian toilets, town houses and churches fell to the developers, many of these architectural gems being reduced to rubble. The intention of course was to replace these with more malls and hotels, which they thought key to the city's identity,' he added sarcastically. 'What was most galling was the fact that most of the population remained ambivalent about it. Anyhow because of my interest in social history I was often asked to talk to groups about heritage matters and so leading on from this I interviewed local resident Jim. He was a font of knowledge and the colourful stories he told from when he was young brought the past alive. I remember showing him some images of an old tram depot once and to my surprise he announced that he had worked there as a young man. His job at the time, he explained, was to deliver leaflets in the vicinity, to help drum up business. This was in the mid-1950s and post-war austerity was still commonplace, and so each day he would leave King Street depot laden with leaflets, posting them along the many streets which ran off the main thoroughfare. There was Roslin Terrace, Pittodrie place, Merkland Road, I'm sure you know them well.' Steve slowly nodded in response.

'Anyhow one day he found himself on Roslin Terrace, a quiet street lined with tenements and on entering one of them walked upstairs. On the first-floor landing sat a girl in a light dress, who was staring ahead of her, she was clutching what Jim thought in retrospect, to be a doll, to her chest. He also recalled that she sat in the middle of the step, as he had to squeeze by her. Something in her demeanor made him unwilling to brush against her and so he turned sideways while passing. Anyhow, as he passed by, he told me he was aware of a distinct chill which emanated from the girl. On reaching the landing above, he glanced backwards only to find she had vanished, which in the time he had looked away, would have been impossible. Dropping the leaflets he left the building hurriedly, the hair on his neck bristling. What had made him so anxious was the fact that the girl he saw had an uncanny resemblance to that of a young girl, brutally murdered in nearby Urquhart Road some twenty years previously.

'I think, I know the case you mean, interjected Steve, but please, go on.'

Alistair, nodded, before continuing. 'I suppose most locals with a passing knowledge of the area would have heard of it, it's certainly infamous. The perpetrator, a jealous neighbour, took the poor lassies' life for unknown reasons, going so far as to brutalize her body to divert attention. This succeeded to a point, although some innocents soon found themselves under the spotlight. It was however one of the first cases which used forensic science and so the murderesses' ruse quickly unraveled. Naturally found guilty, she miraculously escaped the hangman's noose instead receiving a life sentence. The tenement still stands today and is a stones' throw from where Jim worked. He of course was adamant that the girl he saw was the one who had been murdered.'

'But surely that was in an entirely different building?' interrupted Steve moments later. The stranger who up till then had remained passive, smiled slightly to himself and for the first time appeared to show some interest in the conversation. 'Do go on, please.' he murmured, his voice thick with anticipation. Alistair, on noticing his expression, suddenly felt a chill scuttle up his arms and he rubbed them briskly, before continuing.

'Well, those were my thoughts exactly, given that the murder happened in a different location. Well anyway around five years later I was working with another society, this time in the south of the city. One of the participants was an elderly lady, Sheila. We got on to the subject of "grimness" as we used to call it, and of course that story cropped up. To our surprise we found out that that the young girl's mother had been very close to Sheila's mum and used to visit her regularly. The group by now as you can imagine were rapt as the story unfolded, and we were further surprised to be told

107

that the poor woman had visited soon after the incident. Sheila of course, being just a child, had been sent from the room but had overheard everything, as she 'lugged in' from the lobby. It transpired that soon after the murder, the family had decided to move, and who could blame them, but what Sheila couldn't grasp, was why on earth did they choose to move only two streets away, to Roslin Terrace!' A look of mild surprise danced across Steve's features, but the newcomer only nodded.

'Well, that's a conversation killer, or maybe starter,' said Steve, and with that took a sip from his cup. 'Do you think, Jim was being straight with you?'

'I believe he was,' replied Alistair. And with that drained his cup. 'Anyway, that's my story, and it certainly made me think.'

The stranger, up till then a passive participant, now stirred in his seat. 'Well, I just hope the poor lass has found peace,' he murmured. Outside a sudden gust rattled around the building, causing the door to tremble in its frame. The men glanced at each other, before Steve placed another hunk of wood upon embers. Soon after grateful flames lapped at its sides and as the sparks began to sputter into the air, the men drew closer. Mulling their drinks and lost in thought, Alistair was first to break the silence. 'Well as we are all intent on sharing. I think I may have something of interest for you,' and quickly added, 'perhaps afterwards we should set up our own self-help group, like the AA except we can call it GA, Ghosts Anonymous.'

'A great idea, and this is the inaugural meeting,' returned Steve. Chuckling loudly, he surveyed his companions, however the stranger seemed unimpressed by the sudden levity. 'And how are you feeling?' Enquired Alistair suddenly attempting to engage his stoic companion.

'I feel much better now, he countered drily,' though his face belied his assertion.

'Well, that's a positive,' said Steve, with a faint whiff of sarcasm. 'Well as I mentioned I used to work in the third sector, charities, education that sort of thing and always with groups. Anyhow we were based in this bloody awful shoe box attached to a much older building. Our building dated from the 60s and was devoid of any architectural merit unless you like harling. Internally both were connected by a steep central staircase. The premises themselves consisted of a narrow corridor which ran from the front door to a kitchen at the back and off this lay one large meeting room, two bathrooms and an office. You will know the building as its next door to the "Lemon Tree."

Alistair nodded, 'I know the very building I used to wonder what was in there, aah! the mystery has been solved, sorry, do go on.' The narrator continued.

'When I first started working there, I quickly found out that there was something unusual about the building, my colleagues and I felt an acute sense of dread that manifested itself particularly during the winter months. The feeling of being followed by an invisible presence in the corridor was one of the delights we had to contend with, and on more than one occasion when locking up I admit, I bolted for the door. This I must stress was not my imagination. Things took a turn for the worse one morning around two weeks before Christmas. I was key holder that day and on arrival I passed the bathroom as usual. It was then I noticed a woman with long black hair leaning over the sink. She appeared to be washing her hair. I immediately stepped back only to find the bathroom empty. When I told my line manager later that day, she became anxious. To make matters worse we were told by staff from the creche downstairs that they often heard clomping from above after we had left for the night. As you can imagine this only served to make the atmosphere unbearable. In the hope of finding an answer we agreed to uncover the history of the area and so I took on the role of investigator. I must admit I enjoyed the research, but I couldn't turn up anything other than the current building had been built on the site of a plumbers' workshop.

'Terrifying,' crowed Alistair, but a cold glance from the stranger quelled his boisterousness.

Steve continued, 'It was the week before Christmas and our students had gathered for their end of term celebration, nothing spectacular, but tea and cake and some company. It was a tradition within the organisation and if I remember, there were around ten attendees. My boss, interested in hearing about my findings, made some throwaway comments about phantom plumbers on hearing the news, which of course raised a laugh. However, our levity was short lived at the sudden appearance of a creche worker from downstairs, who informed us in breathy tones that water was now pouring through their ceiling from our building. A frantic search revealed the source to be an obsolete shower. Broken for the last five years, it had magically turned itself on the growing puddle testament to a ghostly intervention. I shouldn't laugh but the students vacated the building that day in record time.'

'I don't blame them,' said Alistair. 'Did you ever find out the cause?'

'Funnily enough we did, as soon after my boss asked a medium to visit, to try and find some answers. I don't know what you think of mediums, but it proved to be an interesting experience. It would have been just after New Year in early January, as we were preparing for a new influx of students. It was a cold night as I remember there being ice on the road outside and how difficult it had been to find her a parking space. Anyhow, upon arrival the medium headed straight for the bathroom where I had seen the figure some months earlier and stood for a minute or two, with her hands outstretched. After announcing she sensed the presence of a dark-haired woman, she went on to describe how her head had been shoved into the sink by her partner, also a woman. This malignancy was the cause of the disturbances which she claimed were ingrained in the fabric of the building. In her opinion it had the potential to affect those who worked there so at the end of the evening she performed a blessing. Soon after I moved on to a new job but heard later that the blessing, which temporarily worked began to revert as Winter approached. Anyhow the company eventually gave up the building which is just as well as the atmosphere was awful to say the least. I still can't explain what was happening there but for the record I always left the building rapidly at closing time. The two men shuffled uneasily and for a few moments neither spoke until Steve turned to their silent companion. 'Have you anything you would like to regale us with?' he asked.

The stranger remained as taciturn as before, and an almost embarrassing length of time passed until his soft tones broke the silence. His voice, barely above a whisper now floated in the air and both men lent forward in their chairs, attempting to catch his words.

'Well, I've spent many years walking these hills and have spent many nights in this bothy. Some people like nothing better than being out in the air and the physicality of it draws them to this area. Others, as you know, blanche at the idea of the great outdoors. Over the years I have met many outdoor folk including members of the Cairngorm Club and have been in their company on more than one occasion. Anyhow it goes without saying that this bothy has a reputation amongst climbing fraternities.

'I knew it!' said Steve interrupting the narrative, but the stranger did not acknowledge the comment and carried on.

'People who stay here occasionally come away regretting their decision, and I have known some who would not dare set foot in here at night.

Alistair felt a slight draught tickle at his neck and pulled his collar closer, 'go on,' he indicated with his cup.

'It's haunted so they say, by a who climber died here many years ago. It was, according to reports, a bitterly cold night and the weather had closed in earlier than he had anticipated. This chap, an experienced climber I might add found himself caught with nowhere to go. Perhaps he had been a little naive in thinking he was a match for the land, but I suspect it was a case of the weather turning on a sixpence as it often does. The poor fellow. He reached this very door only to find it locked which it had been since its use as the King's Stables. Two days later he was discovered frozen to death. The king of course was shocked to hear of the tragedy, and so decreed that from then onwards it should remain open. Since that day many have claimed to have seen a man's face looking forlornly into the shelter as darkness fell, while others have witnessed the same figure staring outwards at their approach. Of course, on entering the bothy it was found to be empty. This is quite a common phenomenon, I believe. Others have woken in the night and heard terrible moans as of someone in agony, issuing from the center of the room. Well, that is what I've heard at least.'

'Couldn't someone, have just been playing a prank?' interjected Steve, but the question remained unanswered as the stranger's hypnotic voice continued.

'Perhaps, but I think you will agree with me, that what I'm about to tell you sounds authentic,' and as if to emphasize the point he made eye contact with his two companions. The effect of which they found disquieting, to say the least. 'What I am about to share happened around twenty years ago and involved three experienced walkers. They had hiked all day and with a long walk still ahead of them decided to stop for the night. It was winter and it had snowed heavily. With a further storm now bearing down on them they agreed the best course of action was to split their journey. Of course, the facilities were somewhat more spartan in those days, with guests obliged to sleep across the rafters. I know what you are thinking but unlike the luxury you see today, it was believe it or not a little more basic,' and for the first time since his arrival he allowed himself a half smile. He continued. 'Having gone to bed early, they soon fell asleep. I believe it must have been just after midnight when they awoke to a banging on the door. Roughly dragged from his sleep the eldest of the group shouted out to whoever it was, to let themselves in, but whoever it was appeared unaware and continued to pound the door, now with greater urgency. "Come in!" he cried again in exasperation, yet whoever it was remained outside. Cursing, and with all three now fully awakened, he climbed down from his perch and flung open the door no doubt to give the deaf fool a piece of his mind. Imagine his face when he discovered that there was no one there, I suspect it must have been a picture. Allegedly, the moon which had cast its silvery light across the land revealed nothing, but the snow upon the path virginal and untouched. A quick appraisal of the situation sent them scurrying inside. I suspect they slept little that night.' On finishing a soft chuckle escaped his lips and he stretched backwards with a look of mild contentment on his face.

Alistair shivered and reaching into the basket placed a log on the rapidly dying embers. 'I wish that damn fire would get going, I think the wood must be damp, anyway perhaps we should change the subject.'

'I agree,' said Steve, tipping the now empty flask to his disappointed mouth. The latecomer now rose and stretching fully, let out a sigh, his enormous shadow filling the room. 'If you will excuse me gentlemen,' he murmured, and placing his hand upon the latch stepped outside. They glanced upward drawn out of their reverie by the cold air now rushing into the room. The door was ajar, and a few stray flakes fluttered in. Steve, nearest to the door closed it sharply. 'My God! that's all the heat gone near enough,' and rubbed his hands nearer the flames which were still subdued and reluctant. 'I hope these last a little longer,' he said, indicating the near empty log basket, 'it's going to be a cold night.' His companion concurred and began gathering the last few stray scraps of wood which littered the floor. Once finished, he rummaged in his backpack, seemed to change his mind and then sat back down content to watch the fire now renew.

After several more minutes Alistair broke the silence. 'He's been gone quite a while, don't you think?' Not waiting for a reply quickly donned his jacket and glanced toward his companion.

'I suppose he has,' responded Steve, reading the others expression. Bending down he too quickly pulled on his boots and, grabbing his torch wrenched opened the door. Outside the world had turned silver, a fresh snowfall lay thick on the surrounding trees. The moon stood stark against the sky, its rays illuminating the deep mantle which encased the land. It was still and the snow which lay as far as the eye could see was only punctuated by a few single boney trees. It was surprisingly light and scanning the horizon the desolate landscape revealed nothing of their companion. The men then began shouting into the night but received no response but their own. There was a palpable sense of dread in the air and after exchanging glances both men retreated inside, barring the door as best they could. Later when asked, they described how no footprints had marred the virginal snow which lay thick upon the path leading from the Gelder bothy.

Return to Berkeley Square

I n the private chamber of Judge Mathews sat three men. Mathews, sipping port from an expensive glass had served the law for near 35 years, and although he enjoyed the fruits of his labors, it hadn't dulled his taste for justice. Some might have called him ruthless, though he preferred the term vigorous. He wasn't hugely popular, especially among the criminal fraternity and if anything had a reputation as a 'hanging judge.' Despite sending many to meet their maker, he had never once questioned the fallibility of the system and as such slept like a baby. Opposite sat Richard Devlin, his slight frame engulfed by the chair in which he found himself. He was the younger of the three. At thirty-two he had a reputation as an experienced barrister that far exceeded his relative youth. He was whip smart and something of a celebrity. His child-like countenance disguised a keen intellect as demonstrated by his tenacity in championing the underdog and his enviable record of successes proved this. However, to the detriment of his purse he only defended those he believed to be innocent making him something of a deviant in the eyes of his less altruistic colleagues. Next to him sat, Jacobson, Crown Prosecutor, and although his senior by a mere three years he looked older and mopped at his perspiring brow frequently during the conversation. A clever man, he was pragmatic to a point which made his heart unlike his opponents, considerably smaller. He was in many ways equally matched to Devlin but lacked the others' imagination and ability to deviate from the norm, that had helped build his reputation. At 9.30 am in morning of the 27th of April 1887 the three now sat locked in deep discussion. Mathews' keen to start proceedings had been halted in his tracks by a strange request. The request of course had been submitted formally and now informally he listened. He would never admit to it, but he did have a soft spot for Devlin, despite him being a 'do-gooder.' In respect of this and as a courtesy the meeting now taking place was to stay within the four walls of his somewhat lavish office. The case, which they now discussed had on the face of it started out as a drunken brawl resulting in the death of one unfortunate. Under normal circumstances, the trial and indeed the outcome would have been a foregone conclusion but for one thing, the outlandish claims of the defendant had attracted unwanted attention from the press. Mathews, now grasping said article waved it before him as if swatting flies. 'Really Devlin, this whole thing is turning into a circus, why on earth you have doubts about the man's guilt is beyond me, haunted houses indeed. He should have pleaded temporary insanity, as it is he will more than likely hang unless the jury has been hand-picked for their credulity.'

Devlin stared at the carpet both hands clasping his glass. Seething inwardly, he turned to Mathews. 'I know it sounds ludicrous, but I believe there is more to this than meets the eye and what with the tragic history of the building...'

'History, what history' retorted the judge. 'It's a load of old wives' tales, I'm afraid you best face facts, unless there is a new revelation, Robert Martin will end up incarcerated in an asylum or worse. Which? well we shall soon see, once the evidence is presented. For the record, you have a few days grace to organize the defense. Be careful, if word ever got out you had entertained such fancies, you'd end up a laughingstock of that, I'm sure.' He then turned to Devlin, his face softening slightly. 'Please proceed cautiously, I would hate to see a promising career ruined. Now if you will excuse me gentlemen, I'm expected back home.'

Jacobson, up till then silent, rose and rubbing at his brow grumbled. 'Well for the record I still have my objections, but if it pleases your honor, I will respect my learned colleagues' intentions. I just find the whole thing distasteful, a mere ploy designed to save his clients' neck from the gallows.'

'Perhaps so,' replied the judge, ' but let us not be too eager to send the fellow to his maker just yet, now if you will excuse me, I bid you both a good day.' His guests dutifully obliged and retrieving their coats from the nearby hat stand left.

The neck in question belonged to one Robert Martin, an ordinary seaman aboard HMS Penelope now accused of the murder of his companion and shipmate Edward Blunden. Violent drink fueled arguments among sailors were commonplace and his death would have barely made the papers but for two things, the unusual manner of his demise, having been impaled on a set of railings and secondly the location of the building from which he fell or was pushed, 50

Berkeley Square. The very address synonymous with evil had become known as 'London's Most Haunted House,' with numerous deaths being attributed to the property. Devlin in preparation for the trial had of course trawled the archives and interviewed as many living witnesses as he could find, although unsurprisingly they were thin on the ground. There was also the usual hearsay and supposed eyewitness accounts to sift through however what had got under his skin was the sincerity of the accused. On meeting him, his fragile mental state was apparent and once the story unfolded, he was in no doubt as to its veracity. Devlin convinced of his innocence intended to prove this whether his 'learned' colleague liked it or not. Outside he hailed a cab and within ten minutes it drew up, outside his residence.

Back in his rooms Devlin faced the mirror and straightened his tie. For weeks now he had mulled over the case, debating whether to make a plea for clemency when the time came, or to try and prove Martins innocence. He had decided on the latter. Having already amassed a substantial knowledge of the property long before the case the house had always held a strange fascination for him. Some might have even described it as an obsession, and he would have been a liar if he did not admit to having studied its history in minute detail. Over the years he had amassed numerous accounts from the property, from workmen employed in its repair to former staff and residents, accounts which suggested the building was haunted! The file sitting directly behind him was testament to this and was prodigious in size. Robert Martin, recently brought in screaming hysterically and insisting on his innocence, had further added to the mystery and it was then that Devlin made up his mind to do the unthinkable, to spend a night at 50 Berkeley Square. Of course, the judge would have had him committed at the very idea, but in his mind, it was the only logical course of action. Days had passed since Martins arrest and despite his mounting apprehension it was now or never, the trial set to proceed in two days' time. The house, he was convinced, held a dark secret and he intended to find out what it was.

At around four in the afternoon Devlin's companion for the evening, Frederick Jones, arrived at his home. A past favor had secured his assistance. He had been 'employed' for the evening due to his unique skillset, that of housebreaking, at which of course he was excellent. A handful of coin had further guaranteed his silence, for despite being a thief he was also a man of his word. On answering the door, the furtive figure on the doorstep, removed his cap. 'Evening Mr. Devlin,' he wheezed. Devlin nodded before quickly ushering him into the drawing room, closing the door quietly behind.

'As we are to be companions, at least for tonight, I would be obliged if you would drop the formalities,' said Devlin, please call me George.' On inspection Devlin suspected that his erstwhile guest might be getting cold feet and so immediately presented him with a substantial brandy. 'Lovely,' croaked Fred as the fiery liquid disappeared in one gulp and without the least shame held his glass ahead of him expectantly.

Devlin tilted the decanter in reply, 'Just one more, we will need clear heads if we are going to succeed.' Fred accepted, only withdrawing the glass when the liquid began to rise to an unacceptable level. In the conversation that followed it became clear that despite studiously avoiding the subject of ghosts, Fred had done a little digging himself on receipt of the task. However, the tales of which there were many had little substance in his opinion. Nevertheless Devlin, keen to share more insisted he listened. Dutifully sinking into a nearby chair he looked unimpressed until the decanter was left helpfully near his elbow, it was then that Devlin began.

'The earliest recorded tragedy at the property was the death of a young women whose lifeless body was found smeared on the pavement below the second floor, why she fell remains a mystery, but the popular theory was that she was attempting to flee the brutal machinations of her uncle. By all accounts he was a vile bully who denied all knowledge of her persecutions and escaped unscathed. It was said soon after that the spirit of the unfortunate girl was seen clinging vainly from the window ledge from which she fell to her death. I have no idea if there would be any mention of this in police records, but I suspect not, as it happened many years ago. Despite this, the house did not remain empty for long. Soon afterwards the youngest daughter of the next occupant mysteriously fell down a flight of stairs. Her unquiet spirit is said to have joined that of the previous young woman.'

Fred who had listened without comment then interjected,' Mr. Devlin, I mean George, I know people have allegedly seen these ghosts but what I don't understand is that there is no record of their names or their relationship to them what has died.' Without waiting for Devlin to reply he continued, 'therefore I am of the opinion that these stories are the product of a fevered imagination.' Devlin's brows raised momentarily, before Fred continued. 'And if you don't mind me saying, I am surprised to learn that a man of your background entertains such fancies.'

Now it was Devlin's turn to talk. ' My dear fellow, I entertain such fancies as you say, for a very good reason which I hope to demonstrate tonight.' Fred's eyebrows raised, but Devlin who did not elaborate, ploughed on. In any case, it depends whether the witness can be classed as reliable. Is an educated man more or less likely to lie than an uneducated one? Does a poor man misinterpret an event any differently from that of a rich man? To answer the question, I have found ones' character rather than ones' breeding to be the deciding factor. Take the history of Berkeley square for example. The anecdotal evidence would suggest the building is genuinely haunted and in most instances the witnesses having nothing to gain makes me suspect some truth.' Fred shrugged, glancing hopefully at the nearby decanter, which Devlin now studiously ignored.

'Pray let me continue as there is much more to relate. Around forty years ago one of those rakish louts that populated the squalid drinking taverns of the city doubtless bolstered by ale and a prodigious purse, took it upon himself to demand entry to the said property. The reason, we can only assume, was an attempt to increase his prowess within his social circle, though God only knows who would want to impress such a pack of fools, anyhow he demanded entry. After arousing the bewildered landlord, who resided within two rooms on the ground floor, he made it clear to the man his intentions. He mentioned both his honor and title and when that didn't work produced a purse. Good old-fashioned coin is a great leveler and in due course was invited in on the understanding that he slept with a loaded pistol during his vigil. This he agreed to readily. After ascending to the 2nd floor, an area now semi derelict and shunned by the owner, he was placed in the front bedroom. After some minutes the landlord then retreated to the sanctity of the lower floor no doubt to enjoy an equally sleepless night. It was around 2.30

in the morning when the landlord was alerted by the sound of a single pistol shot and on entering the room found the young bravado in pissed soaked britches cowering against the further wall his gun still pointing ahead. He could not, would not, describe what he had shot at but what little explanation he could give alluded to a shapeless mass that walked through a wall before lunging at him. The young man exited as soon as he could prize himself from the terrified owners grasp and was last seen flying wildly Northward. The landlord we can only assume, wasted little time in bolting himself in for the remainder of the night. Perhaps he was a terrible shot or maybe due to his excessive drinking his aim was off but either way he struck nothing but bare plaster. Others argued that a serious case of delirium tremens was responsible as he enjoyed imbibing ale as others did water.' Fred now silent, indicated with his hand for Devlin to continue.

'Some claimed afterwards that the whole thing was a fabrication, made up to dupe the public, while others argued that it was a cursed house. Others asserted that the restless spirits roaming the corridors were being collected by something demonic, whose origin was unknown. It is also worth noting that the list of formers tenants included public figures, Lords, even a Prime minister, who like the others had his hair raised on more than one occasion. Many believed him beyond reproach, while others because of his occupation smiled wryly, however there can be no denying that what occurred in 1868 was nothing short of sensational.' Devlin stopped momentarily, sipped from his glass, before continuing.

'It is on record that in that year, a family arrived with their servants and set up home. Nothing out of the ordinary occurred for some time and being a pragmatist, the owner held little stock in the local tittle-tattle. That all changed of course, on the day he was alerted by wild shrieks coming from the attic and on investigation found the maid hysterically repeating the words, "Don't let it touch me," "Don't let it touch me." The owners who could do nothing to calm the young woman, called for a doctor who on arrival diagnosed a complete mental breakdown. She suffered the indignity of spending her remaining days in the asylum where she died soon after still unable to describe adequately what she had witnessed. Soon afterwards her betrothed, a commissioned officer, then pleaded with the owner to be allowed to stay overnight in the very room of the tragedy. He was beyond despair, desperate to know the truth and who could blame him. Despite the owners' reservations, it was agreed that he could stay on the condition that they rig up a bell and rope system to ensure his wellbeing. The rope would lead from the room of his vigil to the lower floor where the owner and a few trusted servants would wait. One pull would bring the assembly running, and with just two flights separating them help would arrive within seconds.' Devlin after some moments continued.

'Given the circumstances perhaps a two-man vigil would have been more appropriate, but that is how they played it. At around 2.00 in the morning, they were roused from a fitful doze by the frantic jangling of the bell followed by a single shot. Bursting from the room they plunged up the two flights and upon entering found the unfortunate Captain. A quick inspection revealed a look of wide-eyed terror on his face. He was stone dead. The official report was suicide, but there were no marks upon his body and the trajectory of the bullet found it to be lodged near the window as before.' Devlin sensing his companions resolve falter rose and poured two generous shots, which was gratefully accepted. 'This will be our last till it's over,' he smiled.

'Well Mr. Devlin, you certainly know how to tell a good story, I'm almost beginning to believe it myself.' He quickly gulped the fiery liquid. Devlin's face reddened momentarily and Fred, realizing his faux pas quickly added. 'I would be much obliged if you could tell me again what you expect of me tonight. Just so it's clear in my head, if you know what I mean. It's not so much the thought of ghosts what disturbs me but the idea of which prison we could be residing in should we be caught.'

Devlin afforded himself a slight smile before continuing. 'I have throughout my life explored slightly more outré subjects, shall we say, it's an interest I acquired from my mothers' side of the family. Her ancestry was quite colorful you know. My father, the complete opposite, was a pragmatist and so in effect I have in me the best of both worlds. I am open minded on most subjects and so when given the facts of this case I was intrigued. Martin, my client, though decent, is typically uneducated and has no concept of the otherworldly. In the last few days, I have spent many hours in his company, and he has not once deviated from his story. I mean no disrespect to him when I say this, but he is completely unimaginative and could not invent what he described to me unless he had seen it. When he was first brought in with the smell of cheap whisky upon his breath, his fevered account suggested mental instability and not one person has been prepared to look beyond this. He is not mad, of that I'm certain, but what he saw nearly drove him so. I will now tell you everything I know about the events of that evening and very soon you and I will pay a little visit to the scene of the crime as it were. You, my friend, will then afford us entry. Once inside, all I will require from you is your wits and your obedience. He glanced over at Fred to emphasize his point. Fred, now suitably warmed by the brandy shrugged, 'whatever you say George,' though he remained unconvinced.

Now sitting opposite Devlin began. 'On docking, and with two days of glorious freedom ahead, the ship's company had swarmed into the closest drinking dens on disembarking. 'The Globe' was their first destination where at least twenty crew members downed a few whiskeys of dubious origin. They next frequented 'The Fleece' where the process was repeated. As they made their way along the shore Martin stated the crew then began to split into smaller pockets, some preferring to remain in the docklands while the more adventurous headed inland. After months of sobriety the need to drink was their objective, which they achieved spectacularly. The unfortunate victim Edward Blunden and Robert Martin had become firm friends over the preceding months and according to Martin they had an easy relationship, remaining good-natured even while drunk. This has been verified. At approximately 11.30 that evening and with no idea where they were headed for, neither knew London well, they found themselves in Berkeley Square. How they got there he cannot remember but on arrival the street was quiet. An hour previously, both men had been firm friends with Bacchus but were now sufficiently sober to realize their predicament and with the last of their money guzzled, they had no means of shelter.

It was Blunden who suggested they should try and find a spot nearby and very soon they stumbled across the property which was to be their nemesis. It was boarded up and obviously empty and the men after some moments debate sought egress by the basement. The lower window was found to be unlocked and using Martins' knife they were able to prize it open wide enough to gain entry. The interior, though grand in its day, was now desolate. The downstairs rooms devoid of furniture, retained nothing but curtains and the smell of damp was evident. Martin told me that it was his suggestion they explore further and so after lighting a couple of discarded candles they ventured upstairs. On the second floor, they found four rooms and were pleasantly surprised to note the largest of those contained both a bed and sofa. The floor was also covered by a large rug so at least in appearance it appeared more homely than the others. The decision was then made to make this their home for the night. A toss of the coin then decided who would take the bed. Martin then lit two further candles and placed them on the mantlepiece at either end. As both men were sufficiently sober by then they lay chatting idly about their plans before slowly drifting off to sleep. Sometime later Martin woke to find Blunden's hand pressed across his mouth. Momentarily confused, he witnessed his friend raise a finger to his lips and bade him remain silent. His companion then placed his hand upon his shoulder, his expression one of alarm. The room was noticeably darker, the candles having burnt low, and Blunden's grip tightened as he hissed the word, "Listen." There was a faint sound coming from downstairs and a terrible smell, which he described later as coming from animals in a zoo. Now they both listened. Something was coming up the stairs with steps both ponderous and steady.

Terrifyingly, he described them as sounding like meat being thrown against a wall. Blunden then seized a poker and standing with his back to the fireplace raised it in readiness. The steps had now halted just outside the door which after a moment slowly opened inwards. A nebulous shape now stood framed in the doorway which even now he cannot adequately describe. Consisting of a grey mist a myriad of shapes writhed and billowed within it revealing all manner of horrors, a laughing child's face, the claw of some unspeakable beast, they melded and merged continuously hypnotizing the onlookers. As you can imagine the sight of it near turned Martins veins to ice and being held in its thrall, he found himself unable to move. The pulsating mass now in the room and it was then that the spell broke as Blunden, still holding the poker aloft let out a wild shriek and brought it down upon the thing, with all his might. The pour soul stumbled forward having struck nothing more substantial than smoke and was instantly engulfed. It was only then his companion came to his senses and half crazed with fear launched himself over the settee. Stumbling down the staircase and began clawing at the front door. Stout as it was, it was no match for his feverish hands and was wrenched open within seconds revealing the silent street. He then ran until accosted by a passing policeman before quickly making their way back to the square. What he must have thought on encountering the crazed sailor I cannot imagine, but worse was to come for on arrival they found poor Blunden impaled on the railings directly below the room in which they had slept. The subsequent search revealed no supernatural agency as Martin had claimed and so was promptly arrested. He now feels nothing but shame for his desertion and would happily have taken his friends place in retrospect, God rest his soul.

He has given up and would rather face the hangman to assuage his guilt, but I for one don't intend to let that happen. For your assistance you will be well rewarded and afterwards you will also receive a little extra something for your silence, which I trust you will keep.' He then fixed his companion with a steady gaze. 'Is that clear?'

Taken aback by the intensity of Devlin's stare, Fred nodded. 'Yes, I promise, I will tell no-one. I will do just as you have asked.'

Devlin smiled. 'Good, now if you are ready, we should prepare to leave, I have packed all we will need,' and with that they stepped outside into a waiting cab.

Alighting on the damp cobbles some fifteen minutes later, Devlin glanced upwards and placing his hand on the arm of his companion indicated a recently boarded window on the second floor. Fred nodded silently. To the left of the front door a set of steps led to the basement and at the bottom they stood silently. Above them a lone figure meandered by the tap of his cane slowly receding. A moment later Fred produced a crowbar from within the confines of his jacket and with a skill honed from years of practice jerked the window silently upwards. Devlin was impressed. Inside it appeared most of the windows were either boarded or covered by thick curtains. It was pitch dark and uninhabited for some time; the pungent smell of mildew hung heavy in the air. In the hallway, Devlin rummaged briefly in the bag he carried and on producing two candles quickly lit them before placing them on a nearby table. The light such as it was remained oppressed and so lighting a further two Devlin presented one to his companion before entering what they took to be the drawing room. It was devoid of furniture except for a dust covered bureau on the far wall. Again, he repeated the process of lighting further candles before placing them on the mantle though they did little to dispel the gloom.

A quick inspection of the ground floor revealed nothing more, than drooping wallpaper and a thick layer of dust and so they headed upstairs. The same desolation was prevalent on the first-floor landing and the subsequent rooms which ran off it. After a moments' contemplation Devlin indicated they go on. The 2nd floor was in equally poor shape however the well-proportioned front bedroom boasted a substantial fireplace and to the left of it stood an ancient four poster bed, its legs pock-marked with woodworm. Leaning forward Devlin placed his hands upon the covers. On inspection they were musty though not as bad as he had imagined. Seizing the top cover by its edges he pulled it from the bed and with a flourish draped it over a nearby chaise-longue. 'I suggest when we finish our tour, we should light a fire,' remarked Devlin. 'I'm chilled to the bone.'

'I agree,' said Fred, ' there's no point in us being uncomfortable.' Devlin made no reply. Drinking in their surroundings, his eyes hovered over each surface, nook and cranny. A discarded curtain lay on the floor near a window, now covered with board. The wallpaper or at least what remained of it was yellowed with age, the faded songbird's now ghosts of their former selves. It was an unloved room and it showed. Devlin raised a hand to his temple stood in the silence with head bowed.

'Fred, would you mind getting a fire going, I'm just going upstairs briefly.' Fred shrugged and busied himself gathering fuel. His tuneless whistling was cut short as Devlin closed the door behind him and holding a candle aloft slowly ascended the stairs to the attic. The level of desolation as expected was even worse than below, and it was evident the roof had issues. Plaster littered the floor, and the bare boards were water damaged. Poking his head into the nearest room, he found it empty save for an old cast iron bed. Below the window a small collection of plaster had gathered, and in the air a fetid smell hovered. Stepping backwards he then entered the second room and found it to be worse than the first. A light draught again tickled at is neck and the flame compressing suddenly went out. His nerve almost broke and quickly fumbling for a match, realized he had left them on the mantle. It was then, he heard footsteps approaching. They were soft and quick like that of a child and the flesh on his body began to pucker in response. 'Hello, who are you? I don't mean you any harm,' he whispered, aware of how feeble he sounded, but there was no reply. Outside the moon now risen, bathed the dereliction in silver, revealing the familiar shapes he had observed mere moments ago. He took a step backwards and called again, this time sounding firmer. 'Hello, what's your name?

Seconds later, a soft voice whispered in his ear 'Who are you? The hair on his neck rose accordingly.

After moment's hesitation he replied. 'My name is Devlin, I'm here to try and help a man who is in trouble.' he said softly.

'The man with the cap?' came the childish voice.

'Yes, that's right,' he replied as the hair continuing to rise on his body. 'I'm trying to find out what happened to his friend,' do you know what happened?

There was a moments silence before the voice, now barely audible continued, 'Yes I know, but I won't say, we don't say.'

'Why?' asked Devlin after a moment,

'Because we are afraid of it,' said the voice.

'Of it?' pressed Devlin, 'What do you mean?'

But her tone had grown petulant. ' I won't say, and I don't want to talk anymore.'

There was now only deathly silence, one in which the tiniest sounds can shred nerves and it took a concerted effort for him to not break into a run. He slowly retraced his steps before reaching the landing where he was relieved to find a welcoming shaft of light creeping from under the door. On opening a small fire crackling cheerily in the hearth.

Fred looked up and grinned. ' That's the fire lit! though God knows how much heat it will give off.' Turning his attention to the blaze he then placed another strip of wood across it. 'You were gone some time, is everything alight?' he enquired while continuing to stare into the flames.

'Devlin flopped onto the couch and quickly mopped at his brow. 'Yes Fred, everything is well, I just wanted to get my bearings. How are you feeling?

' A bit knackered to be honest, I think I might have myself a bit of a lie down, if it's all the same to you?' And without permission threw himself onto the bed. Reaching into his pocket he then produced a pouch of tobacco and taking a taper from the fire, lit his cigarette. He then blew a series of impressive blue rings, sighing contentedly as they swirled above him. A brief conversation followed but neither could find the energy to sustain it for too long and so within five minutes it had petered out. Ten minutes later Devlin glanced across to his companion to find him fast asleep. His mouth, slack-jawed, had begun to make a strange rasping sound with each breath and the cap which now covered his eyes rose and fell in sympathy. For the first time that evening Devlin chuckled to himself. Around twenty minutes later he too had succumbed to sleep. It was sometime later that his eyes snapped open and with that he simultaneously eased himself into an upright position. Convinced he had heard something he strained to hear; the silence however remained deafening. He continued to listen convinced that something lay just beyond his hearing. He could now detect a slow insidious thrum, almost subliminal. He listened intently. It was there somewhere in the bowels of the building; he was convinced of it. It was a slow rhythmic pounding, like a muffled heartbeat. A quick glance revealed his companion was still asleep and the hat which had travelled southwards in the intervening minutes now rested on his chin, but this time he did not smile. The candles he observed had also grown smaller and accordingly the light they produced appeared more subdued and the monstrous shadows created by their flame appeared to writhe to the distant pulse.

Rising, he silently tip-toed across to his companion, and placing a hand on his shoulder, shook him gently. Fred remained unresponsive, only waking at Devlin's increased vigor. He rose slowly guided by Devlin's grip, while his eyes darting frantically in their incomprehension. Devlin led him to the mantel, and by the last remnants of the glow they listened. The room was still, but Devlin remained convinced an infinitesimal sound could be heard downstairs and so remained alert. Again, he detected the sound of something slow and ponderous, but this time it appeared to be moving from room to room. 'Don't you hear it?' hissed Devlin.

'I don't hear anything,' whispered his companion in response.

Devlin, looking momentarily baffled, seized him by the collar and repeated the question. 'Open your ears man, don't you hear it? its' coming up the stairs!'

Fred, now squirming under his grip, which had noticeably tightened, looked a little afraid, though Devlin appeared unconcerned. 'Mr. Devlin, I don't hear it, for Gods' sake, listen to yourself, there's nothing there, I can't hear anything.'

Still grasping his companions' lapels, Devlin froze. The second, third, and now fourth step had creaked as if a great weight had been placed upon it. Accompanying the tread was a faint scraping, suggesting the claws of some great beast. The sound grew ominously until at last it stopped outside the door, bringing with it the ghastly smell of corruption. The door bulged imperceptibly inwards and Devlin, now stark with fear, was convinced a mist had now begun to form inside the room.

'Now, do you see? shrieked Devlin, his face contorted in fury. 'There's nothing there I tell you, there is nothing there,' wailed Fred as he struggled to escape his grip. But Devlin, now beyond reason, continued to implore and shriek into his companion's upturned face. Now staggering back and forth in a grotesque dance, the pair clattered against a nearby table sending it crashing to the floor.

'The mist damn you! It's in the room, you must see it, are you blind,' screamed Devlin. If he had hoped for an answer, it was not forthcoming as seconds later an agonizing pain coursed across his companion's chest and with a final gasp, Fred went limp. It was only when the weight of his lifeless body had dragged his crazed companion to the floor, did he relinquish his grip. Shrinking from the others' accusing stare he slowly rose. 'I didn't mean to, it's the house, don't you understand, it's the house,' he mumbled, but Fred, his jaw hanging slackly remained obstinately silent.

A sudden dreadful realisation then dragged him to his senses, having momentarily forgotten his predicament. It was a concentration of evil, unlike anything he had felt, and it now permeated the room. Even the candles once providing a modicum of reassurance now shrank from the malign presence and Devlin now backing away felt his will slowly erode. Staring slack-jawed into the thickening mist he observed what he assumed to be the twisted faces of former residents, writhing in unholy torment. Amongst those were other things too monstrous to comprehend, inhuman things that had never been born yet somehow had been given life through the abomination that swayed before him. Slowly two appendages had now begun to form, the claws of which tapered outwards raking the air as they grew. He prayed, and in those seconds before the first tendril caressed his face his limbs finally unlocked. Leaping to the right and seizing a nearby chair he hurled it with all his might. The missile which instantly passed through the smoky form, exploding violently against the wall but did nothing to slow its progress. Slowly backing away, the cold of the wall now pressed against his spine. It was then he realised he had nowhere to go and the entreaties which followed proved impotent. 'Deny its existence, it feeds on fear!' his inner voice squealed in desperation, but his words like him, were quickly engulfed.

Three days later, a small group of men sat in Judge Mathews private chambers for his customary pre-trial meeting. He slurped noisily from his cup and scowled at the assembly. No one made eye contact except Jacobson who looked very pleased with himself.

'Where, the hell is Devlin?' barked Mathews, rhetorically, as it had already been established that no one knew.

'I have no idea your Honor,' replied Jacobson, 'as I have said no one has heard from him for days. I sent a boy round this morning, but his landlady could not furnish him with any details. I'm afraid it's all a bit of a mystery.'

'Well, he had better make an appearance soon,' barked Mathews, 'the trial begins in two days, and after what we've just been told, it will have to go ahead, with or without him. Anyway, I'm sure there are plenty other prosecutors who would be happy for the opportunity.' The judge wrung his hands which now lay on the table before him nodding gravely.

Jacobson, sipped from his cup, replacing it gently, 'I agree, it must, especially since Martin finally admitted to having murdered his shipmate. And for his purse no less. Hardly surprising.' After a few seconds he continued, 'we can always give it to one of the juniors, it will be a forgone conclusion anyway.'

Mathews rose from his chair and stared from the window at the street below. 'Absolutely, it must go ahead, despite this little show of pique, if that what it is.' He turned to face the room. 'The outcome will be the same either way, ghosts my foot!'

The Girl on the Shore

D onald Sillett stretched back in his chair, a thin curl of smoke drifting from the third cigarette of the morning. In his thirty years' experience as a detective in Aberdeen he had seen it all, and he carried those memories around day in and day out like an overstuffed rucksack. Looking back on his former self he was constantly surprised at how long he had lasted. Domestic violence, GBH eventually graduating to murder he'd done the hours and you could tell by his face. Now soft with age it had begun to droop around his mid-forties though mercifully its journey southwards had slowed by the age of fifty-five. By then a myriad of tiny purple veins had then taken up residence on his nose cultivated by his penchant for drink. Not so long ago he had enjoyed bending elbows with the best of them, but on the death of the traditional boozer he had begun to drink at home, where he frequently unscrewed caps before lying subdued amongst his books and papers. At least his measures were more generous than those in the local hostelries he thought, which was a positive. Today it was all sports bars and pub grub and was a 'bloody disgrace,' in his opinion.

His upbringing had been as hard as the Grey Granite the city was built from. Austerity, they called it, a lifestyle choice so popular it never really went away. He was forthright and unsurprisingly took no shit! An Aberdonian through and through he was decidedly old school and proudly hacked and coughed his way through each day impervious to his younger colleagues attempts to make a new man of him. This "new breed" as he lovingly referred to them, were in his mind a bunch of tattooed, bearded poseurs, hipsters for Gods' Sake! A policeman's duty was to solve crime, and not to look good while doing it he concluded. To add to his irritation, his colleagues viewed him as the grandad of the operation and in doing so took a vested interest in his health with one fresh faced baby even suggesting he should quit smoking. In response Sillett had looked him up and down briefly before letting loose. 'Have you ever thought of fucking off!' Not exactly Oscar Wilde but it had elicited the response he had hoped for. On seeing the youngster's crestfallen face his contemporaries assured him it was 'just Donald's Way.' Donald, as a matter of principle had then quickly nipped out for a fag, cursing the anti-smoking laws which he was loath to uphold. Though often described as contrary, he was respected by his peers though whether he cared or not was a matter of conjecture. He was an enigma.

Outside a light drizzle was now falling and pulling his jacket tighter huddled against the harled surface of Queen Street Police HQ. A van drew up, a horn tooted, and he raised his hand half-heartedly. His mind wandered. He had been thirty years on the force and now found himself increasingly desk bound, caught up in an increasing labyrinth of red tape. He inhaled deeply and a disturbingly loud cough exploded from his lungs.' Bloody weather,' he grumbled and with the cigarette now extinguished he returned inside. The job which he had enjoyed at first eventually cost him his marriage and his ex-wife though still on speaking terms had settled elsewhere. At first, he had found it hard but work pre-occupied him and so had reached the stage in life where he no longer cared for too much company. The process of losing friends as opposed to gaining them had whittled his confidants to a mere handful which also suited him. Returning to his desk he sat heavily down and stared at the image on the screen, some verminous looking chimp had absconded prior to trial and the police were now wasting time on playing hide and seek with him. 'I bet he is loving it,' he thought.

A voice broke his reverie. 'Donald, Inspector Radford wants to see you.' Glancing up he caught sight of his colleague Alan McIntosh, peering from above a bank of screens. He half-heartedly raised his hand in acknowledgment. 'Oh Christ! what now? He groaned inwardly and rising from his chair meandered to the back of the office. In his opinion Radford had been suffering from a terminal case of waiting for his pension for the last ten years, a fact which he did not find endearing. One leisurely stroll later, he reached the inspector's door. Rapping gently upon it he heard a faint mumble and entered. Radford, who half attempted to rise from his desk beckoned him in before sinking back into his chair. Donald entered, all the while studying his superior as if he were a particularly repulsive bug. He didn't like him, never had and made no attempt to disguise it. Radford also contemptuous treated Donald with equal disdain, it was a marriage made in heaven. What irked Donald so, was hard to determine. Perhaps it was the inspectors condescending attitude or his ability to blame others despite his own shortcomings. He also frequently boasted about his ancestral pedigree with each successive generation producing a copper or two. On that point Donald was convinced each had been as ineffectual as the last.

'Hello, do come in, how are you? take a seat please.' Donald dutifully obliged sinking into the soft leather. Once seated, the inspector continued. 'I just wanted to remind you, that you still have a weeks' leave to take before April, so I would be grateful if you can give me some dates as soon as possible.'

'Micro-managing prick!' thought Sillett, outwardly smiling. 'Well, I can take them anytime, Alistair's sorting out the Mckenzie report, so I'm good to go.' Radford nodded and scribbled a few words on the sheet before him.

'Good, good, I will put you down from the 14th to the 28th. Next week then. Have you plans? he enquired, leaning forward.

' I don't know, I have so much choice,' he countered sarcastically.

'Great! good, let me know if you need anything before the weekly briefing.' The inspector continued to scrutinize the Rota and after a moment Donald rose. The meeting was apparently over and so he dutifully returned to his desk. 'Enforced holiday! He called over to McIntosh, who was obviously dying to know the reason for the summons. 'Gossiping bastard,' he thought before smiling in his direction. McIntosh's face had turned a light pink, and he quickly bowed his head to avoid further scrutiny.

Within a few days of being off he quickly found himself at a loss. He knew he functioned better when occupied so holidays enforced or otherwise quickly became a source of agitation. At home he did his best to keep on top of the housework, but as a single man he didn't have to impress anyone other than himself and being easily impressed he did little. In the living room he surveyed his kingdom and concluded that 'Good Housekeeping,' magazine was unlikely to be beating a path to his door anytime soon. It was he concurred, a mess. Bundles of paper, discarded notes and ephemera jockeyed for position across every available surface and his home, once described as generously proportioned, looked cramped. His love of collecting was part of the issue, a mania which his ex-wife had abhorred though the fruits of his labors now lay half hidden in the detritus. At the beginning there had of course been romance and their respective foibles tolerated while under the watchful gaze of cupid. Fifteen years later cupids' arrows had been replaced by poison darts and the marriage annulled. Too many late hours, too much drinking and collecting, were some of the reasons though the list grew increasingly longer with each accusation. At the end, on the day she left, his wife's face looked brighter than it had done in years and that's what had hurt him the most. Afterwards he quickly fell into his old ways, attending auctions and sales filling his home with unloved paper ephemera. These he kept in labelled folders and read over their contents avidly. He was fascinated by the past and his knowledge of the city was unsurpassed. A man needed a hobby, he told himself as continued to add to his collection.

He often wondered what she would have thought, nothing too complimentary he suspected.

On the third day of his holiday, he decided to take a walk towards the shore, around twenty minutes from his flat in nearby Torry. Choosing to walk adjacent to the harbor he drank in its familiarity though the port he had known as a boy had changed beyond recognition. The fishing fleet had for some years been replaced by supply vessels and many of the older buildings he remembered from his youth had been demolished. Lost in thought he briefly stood outside the perimeter gate and observed the harbor basin. It had changed. Not so long ago there had been no fence and generations of kids had happily fished for 'Shitey Sadies,' without killing themselves. But like everything today simple pleasures had been eschewed in favor of health and safety. He closed his eyes and breathed deeply, the unmistakable aroma of tidal wash, seaweed and diesel tickled his nostrils. His mind drifted back to the past and now standing at docks edge he watched its deep green impenetrable surface slowly lapped against its barnacle encrusted pillars. Somewhere in the distance a ships horn honked, and he snapped back to reality his nose mere inches from the grey metal fence. Health and safety gone mad, another of his bugbears. He felt a wave of nostalgia and thought of his father which made him sad. He had been a good man and they had often taken this walk. With a deep sigh he walked on and five minutes later found himself at the harbor entrance. It was evident by the strong breeze that the weather was turning. In the distance foreboding clouds were gathering but as they were some way off, he continued. A quick scramble down the embankment just below the golf course followed before he reached the rocky shore. With each step his feet now sank gratifyingly into the shale. Heading towards Nigg lighthouse, the sound of pop weed crunched underfoot now joined the chorus. His mood lightened and feeling nostalgic bent to pocket a shard of green glass. Turning its smooth surface between thumb and forefinger he let it lie reassuringly in his palm before tucking it away. It was a good find and would soon join its brethren at home where his more interesting finds resided in a jar on the windowsill. One of many they contained colored glass, pebbles and coins all gathered from various walks and he smirked momentarily picturing Annes disapproving frown. Two steps on and his smile abruptly vanished as his ankle twisted. A jolt of pain took him by surprise and gasping he crouched momentarily rubbing his fingers beneath the lip of his boot. After some moments the pain subsided and on straightening up he noticed a girl.

Standing further along the shore she appeared to be preoccupied staring across the harbor mouth towards 'Fittie.' Whatever held her attention kept her rapt and she remained oblivious to his approach. There was something a little 'off' in her demeanor, which he could not explain, and his apprehension grew with each step. They were now literally fifty yards apart and Donald now following her gaze in the hope of being equally enthralled, saw nothing. Seconds later he glanced back to where she had stood but she had gone. 'By God! she moved fast,' he murmured before quickly rubbing his eyes. Above him a gull shrieked mournfully and with an involuntary shudder he quickly retraced his steps.

Later at home he mulled over a cup of tea, it was raining as had been promised. Standing by the window, his nose touching the pane, his thoughts turned to the girl. She had looked oddly familiar, yet he had no idea where he knew her from. Hours later as he rolled into bed, he was convinced he wouldn't sleep, but he was wrong. When morning came, he rose slowly, it was later than he imagined and stepping to the window lifted the blind. The weather, despite the forecast, looked more promising and after a few moments' contemplation dressed quickly. Down in the kitchen he drank the first of two coffees before leaving. Walking briskly for around fifteen minutes he then stood by the water's edge as he had the previous day. A solitary ship bobbed towards the harbor entrance and the sun now at its zenith, was pleasantly warm. For the next hour or so he rooted around on the beach but, finding nothing of interest gave up. Taking a slightly more convoluted route for the return journey he walked past the nearby allotments before veering right. Soft turf soon gave way to tarmac and on reaching Victoria Road he headed towards the old fishery research building. A heat haze hovered above the tarmac, and he stopped to remove his jacket. A moment later he was stopped in his tracks for just ahead stood the same girl from the previous day.

His pace slowed and a sudden nervousness crept upon him sending him fumbling in his pockets. Retrieving the crumpled pack, he lit a cigarette and casually smoked while observing her from his vantage point. As before she appeared lost in contemplation, and he again followed the direction of her gaze. This time her attention was focused on the empty lot which lay between the fishery station and a lone tenement. What held her gaze he mused? There was nothing of interest as far as he could decipher, only a proliferation of weeds and old bricks. Creeping forward he was now around twenty yards from the spot at which she stood and as she remained oblivious to his presence, he was at last able to see her more closely. Maybe it was the heat haze, perhaps his eyes needed testing but either way despite his proximity her appearance remained elusive. She appeared to shimmer or at least that's the only term he could think of to describe her. There was he concluded, something distinctly odd about her appearance. For starters, her hair which was piled high looked out of place, old-fashioned. Her jacket also reminiscent of a style long gone was at least one size too small and sat high on her waist. The shoes, square heeled were tan in color with large buckles on the front. She appeared to be smallish in stature. As for her face, that remained for the moment a mystery. Without warning she stepped into the lot and was instantly lost from view. Donald, who moments before had loitered casually now threw his cigarette down and broke into a run reaching the lot in a matter of seconds. He now stood directly behind the silent figure. He cleared his throat and, excusing himself for the intrusion, raised his hand to touch her shoulder but before he could do so she turned to face him. The color or what little he had drained from his face as he stood and stared.

She was a young woman, snub nosed and with a petulant mouth and he was instantly convinced he had seen her face before, but where? Continuing to stare a voice both broad and couthy slowly penetrated his brain. She unmistakably spoke Doric, the dialect of the north-east, and as the voice probed, her story began to unfold. A strange numbness had now crept across Donald's body, and he found himself unable to move. Her voice ever more insistent began to tell a story that needed to be told, it was her story which had remained unspoken for nigh on seventy years and he was her captive audience. Donald's eyes moistened as the tale unfolded in which she described how she had nebulously existed for decades anchored to the area they now stood in. Why she had remained earthbound quickly became apparent and he felt himself choking back tears of frustration. After several minutes the voice withdrew and Donald, now blinking as if he had come out of a trance stumbled back onto the street.

Afterwards he could not recall the journey home, and it was only after he had gulped two large Gins that some semblance of normality returned. For the first time in his life, he had been rattled by an experience that could not be explained and he felt vulnerable. Used to working with facts, he had dealt with several disturbing cases in his career, but this had infiltrated areas of his psyche which were to say the least, underused. Now sitting at his laptop, he quickly typed in a name, a name that he knew and seconds later an icy jolt shot across his spine as the image of the same petulant young woman appeared on the screen. Perhaps not the most flattering of images it had been taken as a police mugshot after some minor misdemeanor and portrayed a girl forever linked to one of the most horrific unsolved murders in the area. Grabbing a nearby pad he began to take notes and remained at his desk for some hours where after a particularly studious bout of writing noticed the room had grown darker. Springing from his chair he quickly switched on a nearby lamp, his nerves were rattled and for the rest of the night he paced the room unwilling to leave its confines.

At around six in the morning and after a light breakfast he cleared his desk apart from his laptop and sitting down heavily rubbed his face, trying to massage some life into his drooping features. He was exhausted and felt sick, but despite this began scouring his notes, creating a timeline of events. A phone call to the police archivist later in the day added further meat to the story and it was not a pretty one. The girl, synonymous with one of Aberdeen most dreadful unsolved crimes would always remain a grim statistic, a warning to wayward children, a nobody who became a somebody for all the wrong reasons. She had liked to party by all accounts and was known to spend lengthy periods away from home, until that fateful night when she vanished from the face of the earth, never to be seen alive again. The grim discovery of her severed arm on the foreshore of nearby Greyhope bay some days later sparked one of the biggest manhunts ever undertaken in Scotland. Despite multiple sightings of the victim prior to her disappearance, they led nowhere. The case slowly unraveled and despite several good leads and potential suspects, the case remained unsolved. As Donald read, he rubbed at his eyes while a feeling of despondency slowly crept over him, 'what a shit show,' he mumbled, at a loss as to how no one was arrested for the crime. Furthermore, the only piece of evidence in existence, her arm, had been unwittingly destroyed several years back. Perhaps today the outcome would have been different, he mused. At around one in the afternoon exhaustion got the better of him and he briefly lay on the settee where his lids heavy like lead clanged shut. When the sudden jolt which brought him back to reality occurred, he was somewhat taken aback to find the room was in near darkness. Fumbling for his watch, the illuminated face showed the time to be approaching 3.30. Astonished he reached for the now cold coffee at his side and took a gulp. It tasted bloody awful, and he put it down with a look of disgust. He rose and approaching the front door pulled on his coat before leaving the house. Why did he leave, he had no idea but nevertheless he felt compelled to do so. Outside, the street was deserted and pulling his coat tighter he walked quickly towards town. He felt out of control, compelled to go there, but why? He was now walking adjacent to the harbor, the familiar hum of the docked boats now providing an accompaniment to his strangely staccato footsteps. A palpable sense of dread now manifested itself and despite attempting to go back he was driven forward as if by some outside agency.

Now standing on the corner of Market Street, and despite the lateness of the hour, he was astonished to find the nearby streets bustling with cars and people. He quickly crossed the road at the intersection and after lighting a cigarette and made his way inside a brightly lit pub. Which bar it was he could not tell but he drawn by the lights and revelry. Inside the atmosphere was raucous, discordant, and the twisted faces of the clientele moved in and out of his focus as they sang and laughed. They were poorly dressed, poverty stricken and despite their jocularity there was a sense of tangible desperation in the air. Desperation to have a good time and to forget. A mantel stood to the right and on the fire a shovel containing 'Buckies' sizzled. The air was thick with smoke and through this miasma a man smiled at him. He had thinning hair, a small moustache and very bad teeth but somehow Donald knew him. He then found himself leaning forward and clutched at the man's sleeve. The man grinned like and shark and placing his hand on top of Donald's gave it a light squeeze. It felt reptilian and Donald shrank from his touch. Nothing felt right and with mounting panic realized that his hand now encased by the stranger's grip was chubby and red. It was skin that had spent too much time in water and though it appeared to be his own he didn't recognize it. There was also a distinct smell of fish in the air which only added to his queasiness. Swilling his drink, Donald felt his stomach growling though lack of food exacerbated by the fiery liquid now running towards it. He stood up suddenly feeling sick, but an insistent hand pulled him down. He rose again and this time shoved the man away before staggering from his chair and lurched to the bathroom. His head reeled, he felt as if he had been drugged but that was impossible. Inside the toilet was dingy and illuminated by a single bulb. Leaning over he splashed his face with tepid water before looking in the mirror, staring back at him was the face of the petulant teen. Gasping for breath he burst from the bathroom but was seized before he got far and persuaded to rejoin the table. He sat down heavily. The man opposite smirked his condemned house smile and pushed another drink forward which Donald was compelled to accept. Two sailors had now begun to argue and the landlady who possessed arms like hams seized the taller of the two and whispered a sweet something his ear. What was said was anyone's guess, but it had the desired effect and afterwards he sat as if in church. The noise, which up till that point had been unbearable suddenly ceased and with it the image of the company slowly faded. Perhaps he had fainted, but a cold blast of air quickly brought him to his senses.

He was now back on Market Street, leaning against a nearby wall when he felt an arm go around his shoulders. He wanted to run but Donald, now a prisoner inside the body of the girl, was powerless and a feeling of mounting dread surged through his every fibre, as one foot was placed in front of another. He glanced fearfully to the left and the man with the bad teeth smiled a predatory smile, tightening his grip with each step. Donald was now being half carried up Victoria Road, he recognized the street, but it looked different somehow and he intrinsically knew they were nearing their destination. Flinging himself to the left Donald attempted to break free, but his companion held him in a vice-like grip until at last the interminable journey stopped. Ahead of them loomed a tall dark tenement and although Donald couldn't recollect the building, he instinctively knew he had been there before. It seemed oddly familiar and then it dawned on him it was the location of the lot. His head drooped momentarily and upon waking found himself within a room, a single lightbulb illuminating the poverty of the surroundings. The furniture which was of universally poor quality sat randomly across the room and was buried beneath piles of discarded bottles and household waste. In the recess the bed lay unmade, the sheets a dirty grey. What little ornamentation there was, consisted of nick knacks of the most abominable kind. The light barely casting a glow revealed nothing of the rooms' furthest recesses, which were no doubt equally vile. The man now busied himself straightening the covers, then poured two drinks from a nearby bottle. Donald's hand attempted to push back the proffered drink but on further insistence it was taken. It was bitter and vile, and Donald gagged. The man smirked and pulled his chair closer. His hand now sat firmly on his knee and Donald attempted to push it away but could not find the strength to do so, only then realising the danger he was in. The light dimmed, momentarily returning only to reveal a dreadful tableau, as a series of wild shrieks exploded in his ears. It was then the true nature of 'her,' friend was revealed, and Donald now witness to what was unfolding stood impotently unable to move or avert his gaze. The man his face a mask of fear and debauchery now hovered above the young girl's prone body, the over enthusiastic blow which she received leaving Donald in no doubt as to her condition. A surge of anger kicked in and without thinking Donald sprang, though quite what he hoped to achieve remained unanswered as on lunging forward to seize the miscreant he caught nothing but thin air. Awakening with a start he found himself sitting upright at his desk, mere inches away from the image of the deceased girl who continued to stare from the monitor.

With only a few days remaining of his holiday Donald took the decision to phone in sick. It was a lie of course but he didn't particularly care and Radford, no doubt happy to be spared his company for a little longer, did not press the matter. Perhaps Donald was beginning to get a taste for civilian life he secretly hoped. After phoning Donald retreated to the bathroom and glancing briefly into the mirror, his reflection revealed what he had suspected, he looked like shit. Throwing some water onto his face, he patted it dry and looked again hoping for a miracle, but none was forthcoming. After boiling the kettle he made coffee and in a moment of absent mindedness took an almighty gulp, the resulting eruption spraying from his mouth.

Concluding that whatever horrors had been perpetrated against her were now being shared, with or without his permission, he nevertheless accepted the burden. An inner knowing now coursed through his being and for the first-time years he felt strangely content. What little sleep he had was punctuated with study, yet he felt more alive than he had done in years. It was apparent that the chief suspect had escaped justice due to lack of evidence. He would of course be long dead, but if the suspect was named, then perhaps…. peace? Later that evening he sat silently in the living room a single lamp illuminating the room. At six he had poured the first of four stiff drinks and in the ensuing hour, his mood had gone from one of anxiety to that of mild bravado. He rose shakily from the sofa and went to fetch another, before grabbing a duvet from the cupboard. Taking a sip, he then cocooned himself on the sofa where he stared fixedly at the lampshade above. It was dusty and he wondered what his wife would have thought of his housekeeping skills. She had frequently called him a messy bastard and in his stupor made a half-baked promise to repent. After some minutes he closed his eyes.

Opening his eyes, he found himself standing inside a dilapidated outhouse. The whitewashed walls and boiler were like those he grew up with but instead of nostalgia felt only impending dread. Watching voyeuristically from his vantage point he could see the back garden and surrounding tenements. It was when the temperature had plunged significantly that he knew he was not alone as the girl now stood behind him. 'Look.' She whispered and Donald's eyes were drawn to the back door of the property. Seconds later a short burst of wild screaming punctuated the night. Ending as abruptly as it had begun, the noise had brought no response from the surrounding buildings. It was then an involuntary tear of shame coursed down his cheek. A terrible feeling of helplessness now engulfed him before a consolatory hand was placed on his shoulder. A moment later they stood together now looking through the window. As before the room was shambolic. Now pulling a battered case from beneath the table, the murderer opened it to reveal a long roll of rubber and after further deliberation began to drag furniture from the center of the room. With the floor now empty he then spread the rubber sheet onto the floor before taking a hefty swig from a nearby bottle. Removing his jacket, he then rolled his sleeves up. The body, which thankfully had remained obscured by a nearby table, was then clumsily hauled onto the mat. Standing up the man drew a greasy wrist across his forehead before disappearing into the lobby. After what seemed an interminable time, he returned with a tool bag and within it produced a saw. Donald, aware of what was about to unfold, shrank from the sight, but the pressure of her hand invited his gaze. Barely able to look, he was relieved to see that a trunk now stood in the center of the room and all that had transpired was over.

It was only then the presence of the girl withdrew leaving him alone, with a bitter ache gnawing at his insides. looking more deviant than before with two days growth upon his chin the killer had now been joined by a better dressed man who appeared to be admonishing him. Gesturing on more than one occasion towards the trunk he paced the room before seizing the others' lapels and shoving him to the ground. The shabbier of the two arose like a beaten dog before slinking to the nearby table where he poured two drinks. After a moment's consideration his companion accepted the glass, gulped it down before leaving the room. Later the well-dressed man re-appeared who in the interim had changed his clothes, now wearing a dark jacket. After a brief conversation the pair seized the trunk and between them manhandled it into the back of a waiting car. The car sputtered into life and after taking the first left at the end of the road headed downhill towards the harbor maneuvered itself towards the waters' edge. There it quietly ground to a halt. In the dark the water which lapped at the harbor's edge had the appearance of treacle. Behind them on the brow of the hill the tenements they had just left sat stark and silent. Christ didn't anyone use lights on back then, sighed Donald? But his question remained unanswered. His attention was then drawn to the soft click of the boot opening. Grunting and gasping the two men now began manhandling the case to the water's edge where they stood whispering and glancing fearfully towards the nearby houses, but all was still. Spared the sight of the last indignity, Donald then felt himself slowly drawn backwards as the scene faded. Afterwards it took several minutes before he regained his senses and with an overwhelming sense of relief slept soundly for the first time in years.

When he awoke it was nearly eleven and it was with a supreme effort that he had to drag himself from the comfort of his bed. Once dressed he retrieved a notepad and over the course of the next few hours harassed the archivist at the local authority records office. A list of names of residents at the suspect's address was duly provided. He then called in to the police archives where with the promise of a few jars secured the help of John Rae who was more than happy to oblige. Being of a similar vintage he had known Donald for years and so took little persuading. A file duly appeared though it was apparent that it had not been opened in years. Containing nothing more than what was already in the public domain Donald's heart sank until tucked at the back a second smaller envelope was revealed. The grubby envelope, to Donald's surprise, contained a list of names. They had been scribbled with little due care and attention onto a scrap of paper and partially glued to the preceding page therefore making it difficult to decipher. On borrowing a magnifying glass, however, things became literally clearer. The archivist carefully extricated the paper and turned a blind eye allowing Donald to scrutinize the contents at his leisure. Donald quickly noted the names and on the fourth his eyes widened.

'Did you get everything you needed?' enquired John, on his colleague's departure sometime later. 'Aye John, I certainly did, and I'm much obliged.' He shook the startled archivist's hand firmly and after promising a drink or two in the forthcoming weeks hurriedly left. Back at home he spread his findings on the table before him. One of the names was particularly intriguing, being an identical surname to that of a former resident of number fifty-eight, later demolished to make way for the fisheries office. He looked up from his desk and for the first since God knows when afforded himself a brief smile.

On Monday morning Inspector Radford, on arriving at work, was taken by surprise to find Donald slouched at his desk. 'Good morning, Donald, I didn't expect you back so soon,' he said with some hesitancy. Receiving no reply, he pressed on. 'Are you, all right, you look a little tired?'

'I am little to be honest, I just wondered if I might have a quick word, it's quite important!' And with that offered a weak smile.

Radford somewhat puzzled, kept a straight face. 'Very well, I can spare you ten minutes, if you would like to come in now,' and he held the door open cordially, despite his expression.

'Please take a seat,' indicated the inspector once inside and Donald obliged. Although acutely aware of the inspectors' scrutiny he wanted to savor the moment and so it took several minutes before he pulled out a faded document.

Donald cleared his throat, before speaking. 'If you don't mind, I will get to the point as I know you're busy,' he said, trying not to sound sarcastic for once. Radford's features remained impassive. 'I was at a bit of a loss to find something to do during my holiday, so I began to look at a few old cases relating to the city, just for fun you understand,' Radford remained silent, a finger now resting on his chin. 'Well, I started to look at the Hadden case, its' always intrigued me, particularly as it's never been solved. Do you know the one?' 'Of course, its Aberdeen's most notorious unsolved murder,' countered his superior.

Satisfied, Donald continued. 'Anyhow, as I mentioned, I needed a wee project to keep myself busy, so I decided to visit the archives. I don't know if you've been, but they're such helpful folk. Radford shifted in his chair, the leather squeaking in protest. Donald continued. 'As a fellow policeman I found out a few hitherto unknown facts you might find interesting.'

Radford who up till then had appeared nonplussed suddenly became animated 'My God, Donald, you don't believe in relaxation, do you? Couldn't you have let work alone, at least for a few weeks.' Donald did not respond. 'Well carry on then I'm all ears,' barked the inspector, after the silence became unbearable.

Donald glanced up from his papers and continued. 'A name turned up, a prime suspect as it were. He went by the name of Radford. Were you aware?' At the mention of his name, Donald noticed the inspectors jaw twitch visibly. Quickly regaining his composure Radford indicated for him to continue.

'James Radford or Jimmy as he was known, kept bad company and was known to the victim. His home, near the top of Victoria Road is now gone I'm afraid. It was a tenement, one of those demolished to make way for the fisheries complex. I even have his house number, if you're interested. Did you know about this? I assumed you might have. Of course, I cannot prove it's him having been dead for over fifty years. Apparently, officers at the time were so convinced of his guilt that they watched him for months just in case he made a wrong move. He must have had a very guilty conscience as its on record, that he kept his lights on twenty-four-seven. I wonder why.'

Radford interrupted, 'that's all very interesting, but it's common knowledge, I am, familiar with the case you know, one would have had to have been living in a hole not to. There is nothing you have told me that's not already public knowledge. Now if you don't mind, I must get on.'

Donald remained seated. 'There is one more thing. I inadvertently came across a scrap of paper with some names on it during my investigation. James of course was on it but surprisingly so was his brother Alfred. Did you know about him?' The inspectors face paled, but Donald pressed on. 'Unlike James, Alfred had done very well for himself, correct me if I'm wrong wasn't he an inspector in the police force at the time?' Radford made no reply. 'I believe he was your grandfather.' Radford remained silent. 'Is it possible he may have suppressed evidence because of the family connection? Maybe he did a hell of a lot more than that, and if so, I intend to prove it!'

With barely concealed fury Radford's half rose from his chair and jabbed a finger at his subordinate. 'How dare you! You spiteful bastard, coming here making wild accusations, and to what purpose? Everyone involved is long dead, the case is unsolved and will remain so. My grandfather did have a brother, and yes, he was a suspect, but it never reached court. Why? Because of lack of evidence. I am warning you, if you continue with this fantasy in any way shape or form, I can assure you I will take legal action. You are a troublemaker and always have been, you're venomous and bitter, perhaps you should consider retiring while you still have a pension! How long have you been here now, 35 years? I recommend you do so.

Despite the barrage Donald remained impassive, he had the upper hand and knew it. How satisfying it was to see Radford turn the color that he had. He knew he had him on the ropes and naturally pressed home his advantage, 'you can have my resignation as of today, I've had my fill of this place and its politics,' and rising slowly he bade his colleague good day grinning as he did so.

Afterwards, the office whisperers were somewhat surprised to hear the news of Donald's impending retirement, but concluded it was probably for the best. Donald, who for once concurred had already begun composing a resignation letter. After thirty-five years, he could cope for a few more weeks and would no doubt be given light desk duties to help speed him on his way but didn't care. His colleagues, those he counted as friends rallied round and though he didn't want a fuss, a date was set for a night out. Donald was delighted to learn it would be in "the Grill". Like the men who drank there it had a pedigree which Donald found appealing. Later that evening he took a walk to the foreshore, it was a calm evening and a lone ship bucked on the swell before leaving the shelter of the breakwater. The shoreline was empty and as he trudged ahead, he felt aimless, almost carefree. He kicked a pebble and stood for a while thinking about the girl but could not feel her presence. Perhaps she had found peace, but just in case he knew what he must do. Back home he sat at his desk and began to write her story.